Stage Fright

or

"LAUGH?" I Thought I'd DIE!

An Evening of Screams.
With Laughter.

by Todd McGinnis

Baker's Plays
c/o Samuel French, Inc.
45 West 25th Street
New York, NY 10010
bakersplays.com

STAGE FRIGHT OR LAUGH? I THOUGHT I'D DIE! was originally produced by Scott Lale, Artistic Director of the Brampton Theatre Production Office, assisted by Danny Harvey, and debuted in October 2001, just in time for Halloween. The cast was as follows:

SANDRA/CIGARETTE GIRL/LISA . . . . Sarah Title

MONSTER/ACCOUNTANT/THOMAS FOX . . . . Rob Woodcock

GERALD/PRESTO/TERRY/MARTIN . . . . Ryan Gladstone

JIM/TOM/JIMMY . . . . Robin Cunningham

PHIL/CORWIN HAYGOOD/P.A. . . . . Reston Williams

EVELYN/SET DRESSER/JENNA . . . . Melanie Windle

ROGER EVERETT/SVEN IVERSON . . . . Peter Richards

CHARACTERS

Act 1, Scene 1, "NIGHT CALLS" – (1F/5M)

VOICE OF CHARLOTTE – child's voice, female, the ghost of a little girl

VOICE OF EVELYN – female voice only (She appears in Act 1 Scene 2; her description is there.)

SANDRA – female, a stage actress

VOICE ON PHONE – male voice, evil, demonic

MONSTER – male, a stage actor

GERALD – male, an affected, arrogant, irritable stage director

PHIL – male, is heard shouting from the tech booth/back of the house

JIM – male, a stage hand

Act 1 Scene 2, "PRESTO" – (4F/4M)

CORWIN HAYGOOD – male, slick, rich-voiced announcer in the "Golden Age of Radio" (Note: character returns as "ACTOR" in Act 2, Scene 1.)

PRESTO – male, a stage magician and mentalist, the "Amazing Kreskin" or "Derren Brown" of his day

ROGER – male, a businessman enjoying a "night on the town"

TOM – male, a skeptic

EVELYN – female, an affluent woman with an infectious laugh and a dark secret

CIGARETTE GIRL – a sexy cue-card girl for Corwin's radio broadcast

CHARLOTTE – child, female, the ghost of a little girl (may appear onstage or be heard as Voice-only)

LUCRECIA – female, Presto's assistant, no dialogue

Act 2, Scene 1, "SOLILOQUY" – (4F/4M)

P.A. – male/female, loud and "bitchy," a film production assistant in charge of the extras on a movie shoot

IAN – male, Production Accountant for the movie production company

JIMMY – male, a technician for the theater on loan to the film shoot

SET DRESSER – female, a cranky, militant anti-smoker

ACTOR – male, a senior (This is Corwin Haygood as a much, much older man.)

WRANGLER – male/female, in charge of various creepy critters on-hand for the movie

TERRY – male, motion picture director, nice guy under a lot of pressure.

SCRIPT GIRL – female, a script assistant on the production

Act 2, Scene 2, "HAPPY HALLOWEEN" (1F/3M)

JENNA – female, a driven, savvy real estate agent

THOMAS FOX – male, a senior, the grown son of Jim, the stagehand from Act 1, Scene 1

MARTIN – male, Jenna's male friend

THE JUGGLER – male (This is the scary, silent performer in the "Alice Cooper"-style face paint who performs for the audience before the show begins.)

SETTING

The Orpheus Theatre

TIME

Spans from the early 20th to early 21st centuries as noted below.

Except for Act 1, Scene 2, which must take place in a year when Halloween fell on a Saturday, every effort has been taken to give directors the greatest possible flexibility with respect to the years in which each scene might be set.

Act 1, Scene 1, "NIGHT CALLS" – mid-1950's to 1969.
Act 1 Scene 2, "PRESTO" – 1937 (though '43 or '48 might also be used)
Act 2, Scene 1, "SOLILOQUY" – mid-1980's or at the end of the 1990's
Act 2, Scene 2, "HAPPY HALLOWEEN" – some time after Act 2, Scene 1

ACKNOWLEDGMENTS

The Author wishes to acknowledge Scott Lale, who created the opportunity to bring this work to life, and all the cast and crew of the premiere production.

AUTHOR'S NOTES

In writing courses of all stripes across the land you will hear this mantra: "Show me, don't tell me."

In the proper context, it's excellent advice and helps one avoid unnecessary exposition in dialogue.

However, as with any pithily phrased "truism" or "rule" it's authority is not absolute, nor is it applicable or even desirable in all circumstances.

For example, when have you ever heard anyone say "Let's get together and SHOW ghost stories around the campfire." The answer of course is: Never.

The art form is called Story*telling* for a reason.

The power of one person telling something to another, informing them, challenging them, making them laugh or best of all…safely scaring the heck out of them, when passion and commitment fuel the endeavor there are few things more compelling.

Don't worry, there's lots of showing to be done in *Stage Fright*.

But the fundamental inspiration for this play was the *telling*.

Tell it well and your audience with thank you with gasps and giggles.

Give 'em Hell!

-TMcG
January 17, 2012

This play is dedicated to my family: my parents Tim and Noreen McGinnis; my grandparents Harry and Annie Bawden and Tom (a natural storyteller) and Mattie McGinnis; my brother Mark, sister-in-law Anne, and nephews Patrick and Brian; and of course, my lovely wife and partner in crime Tracy McGinnis, with gratitude for the many ways they have shown their support over the years and influenced the person I am.

And most importantly, I dedicate this play to my other brother Jim Martherus, lifelong friend and the first person with whom I was able to share my absolute love of horror and fascination with fear and things that go bump in the night. The creepiest parts of this one are for you, buddy.

BEFORE THE PLAY BEGINS...

(As the audience enters the lobby, they encounter a scary looking **MAGICIAN** *wearing Alice Cooper-ish greasepaint makeup. He does not speak to anyone. Not to explain, or engage, or entertain. He silently performs his sleight-of-hand [or possibly juggling or fire-eating] trick, then takes a bow and moves on. His objective is simply to be seen by and to slightly unnerve as much of the audience as possible before the show.)*

(He is a ghost that only the audience can see. They will eventually learn that he is the dark spirit who haunts the Orpheus Theater.)

(If he must perform in the house itself he should do so in the aisles and/or in front of the stage…not on it. The trappings of the production must not touch on him or acknowledge his presence in any way. This includes personnel.)

(If he is in the house itself he must leave at least a few minutes before the house-lights dim.)

ACT 1

Scene One

NIGHT CALLS

(in darkness)

(SFX: the whispering voices of Lotty, a little girl, and Evelyn, a woman, intertwined and overlapping)

LOTTY. *(V.O.)* It was mama's fault…it was all mama's fault… if only she could have – why wasn't she…? Why did she have to…? *(bursts into inconsolable sobs and crying)*

EVELYN. *(V.O.) (hysterical sobbing)* …no NO *NO!* My baby! No… *(degenerates into more sobs, unintelligible murmurs and repetitions)*

(SFX: More voices join with Evelyn's. Moaning and muttering softly, pained. And even more Whispering Voices join, a veritable chorus of them, men and women, too many to make out what any of them are saying. The Whispering Voices drown out all other recognizable voices as the volume increases, swelling to an almost painful crescendo then cut off, suddenly, by a sound like a gust of wind or a terrified, gasping intake of breath.)

(silence, for at least 6 beats)

(SFX: A sudden smack of thunder shatters the silence.)

(And a flash of lightning briefly illuminates…)

(Our stage: There are two free-standing doors, one upstage right, the other stage left. There are no walls. Up center is a kitchen table with a single place-setting. A wall is suggested by a window frame, hung with curtains, which is suspended right of center between the table and the stage left door. Down right, an old-fashioned, rotary dial telephone occupies a small table.)

(The moment passes. Darkness.)

(SFX: We hear the deep ticking of a grandfather clock and the muffled sound of a steady rainfall outside. After a few moments we also hear a low rumble of distant thunder. The clock continues to tick.)

(There is a dull flicker of lightning, too brief and weak to actually illuminate much of anything onstage. It is followed a moment later by…)

(SFX: another, louder roll of thunder. The clock ticks.)

(There is another lightning flash – longer and much brighter this time, enough to illuminate the scene – accompanied by…)

(SFX: a very loud thunder crash.)

(SFX: The clock chimes midnight, unnaturally loud, as thunder continues to rumble and lightning flickers. Then, after the twelfth stroke…)

(There is a very loud knocking at the stage left door.)

*(Enter **SANDRA**, right, in a housecoat and carrying an oil lantern.)*

SANDRA. *(calling out)* Who is it?

*(The pounding at the door continues as **SANDRA** crosses left, pausing to look out the window and see who it is. She can't and continues towards the door.)*

I'm coming. I'm coming…

(She opens the door… There is nobody there.)

(peering and calling out into the darknes.) Who is it? Who's out there? *(annoyed)* Bobby Chase is that you?…Well you can bet your *mother's* going to hear about this!"

*(**SANDRA** slams the door, annoyed and stands a moment, hand resting on the doorknob.)*

Of all the stupid, childish…

(She takes a few deep breaths to calm herself, heaves a final, resigned sigh and…)

(A telephone rings loudly.)

*(**SANDRA** jumps, letting out a startled scream, then quickly settles back down to annoyance. She crosses to the phone and picks it up.)*

SANDRA. *(cont.)* Hello?

(Sfx: the faintest sound of male breathing on the other end of the line)

Hello?

*(Just the breathing. **SANDRA** stares at the phone for a moment, then hangs up. She looks at the door, then picks up the phone, dials and waits.)*

Hello? May I speak to John Turbott, please…Yes, this is his wife calling…I'm fine, Bill. How are you?…No, I'd rather hold if you don't mind…Thank you.

(lightning flash /SFX: thunder crash)

(trying to sound casual) Hello…No, no. There's nothing wrong…You didn't call here a few minutes ago did you?…Oh…No. I'm fine. I just wanted to know if you were coming home soon. You'd said you didn't know if Dennis would want you to – …Oh, that's good. Well, I'll see you when you get home then…No. I can't sleep. The storm I guess. I'll heat your dinner up…Yes. I'm fine…See you soon.

(Calmed, she hangs up the phone. She sighs, relieved…)

(Wham wham wham! Pounding at the door.)

(Startled, she is hesitant to move. She takes a butter-knife from the kitchen-table before approaching the door, cautiously. She reaches for the doorknob, very slowly…Then, just before her hand can touch it…)

(Wham wham wham! At the door.)

*(**SANDRA** jumps back, gasping. Slowly, she recovers. Then, determined, she takes a few deep breaths, steels herself against her own apprehension and raises the arm that holds the knife. She reaches out, grasps the door-knob, takes one deep breath and…)*

(The phone rings again!)

*(***SANDRA*** *screams, leaping away from the door. She crosses to the phone and picks it up.)*

SANDRA. *(cont.) WHAT DO YOU WANT!?!"* *(suddenly sighs, relieved)* Oh, it's you. Thank *goodness*…No. No, I'm fine. It's just, some of the local *brats* are out playing *nicky-nicky-nine-doors.* No…no…it'll be alright, I – What?… Oh. He did. Well, do you have to?…No. No, you're right. We need the money. I'm just being silly anyway. It's just those miserable kids got me all worked up. But they've probably gotten tired of it already…I'll be fine. Sure. I'll see you in the morning…Bye.

(She hangs up and…the phone rings immediately. She starts, then, realizing it will be her husband calling back, smiles at herself and picks it up.)

That was quick. Did you forget something?

VOICE. *(V.O.)* Did *you?*

SANDRA. WHO *IS* THIS?

VOICE. *(V.O.)* Why don't you open the door and find out?

SANDRA. Look! I don't know who you are, or what kind of game you think you're playing but I've had enough! I'm hanging up now and calling the police! Do you understand me? Now stop calling here!

VOICE. *(V.O.)* If you want this to end why don't you just open the door?

SANDRA. …Because every time I do…there's no one there.

VOICE. *(V.O.)* There's someone there this time…

*(***SANDRA***, uncertain, looks nervously at the stage left door.)*

SANDRA. Oh, I'm sure there is! And I'm sure he's ready to knock on the door and run away again just as soon as I *hang up on you! Isn't he?* You coward. You're nothing but a *coward!* *(screams at the stage left door) Both of you!*

VOICE. *(V.O.)* Why don't you go see for yourself? I'll stay on the line…I promise.

(**SANDRA** *sets the receiver down and, taking her butter-knife with her, once again apprehensively approaches the door. Then when she's only a few feet from it…wham wham wham! But she was ready for it this time and strides right to the door, determined, knife raised.*)

SANDRA. *(cont.)* I've got you this time!

(*She throws open the door…There is no one there.*)

(*screaming into the dark*) How are you doing that? *(then at the phone from where she's standing)* How are you doing that?

(*She crosses to pick up the phone, leaving the door open behind her.*)

I *told you* there'd be nobody there. It's just like I said. *You're cowards!*

VOICE. *(V.O.)* You answered the wrong door.

(**SANDRA** *freezes, her eyes widening with terror.*)

(*Lightning flashes SFX: Thunder explodes right on top of it.*)

…It's the *cellar* door he's waiting behind…

(*Slowly* **SANDRA** *looks over her shoulder at the door up right, the receiver slipping from her hand.*)

That's right…go on…He's waiting for you…

(**SANDRA** *raises the knife and slowly approaches the door.*)

Yes…that's right…go on…nothing to be afraid of…

(**SANDRA** *reaches for the door handle.*)

It will all be over soon… *(begins to chuckle)*

(**SANDRA** *draws the knife back, ready to strike, then throws the door open to reveal…NOTHING. Only blackness.*)

(**VOICE** *is cackling, insanely.*)

(**SANDRA** *whirls about and storms back to snatch up the phone…*)

SANDRA. I'm going to get you for this! Do you hear me?

(Behind her, the opened cellar door begins to swing slowly closed, revealing a ghastly, ghoulish-looking man who is now somehow standing behind it.)

I'm going to find out who you are! You just see if I don't…

(The **VOICE** *continues to cackle, and the ghoul behind the door begins to begins to shuffle slowly towards her, sneaking up on her from behind, reaching out for her neck.)*

(unaware of the monster approaching behind her) …And when I do you're going to be sorry you ever decided to play this little game with *me! The police can trace these calls you know!* They can! I called them, you know… They're probably listening *right now!*

(Just as the monster is about to grasp **SANDRA**'s *throat… the "lightning" begins to flicker on and off in a rapid and most unnatural manner and the phone begins to ring, sustainedly.* **SANDRA** *the actress drops character.)*

Oh god. Not *again!*

(Another burst of phone-ringing.)

(out over the house, to someone in the control booth) Hel-*lo?* Why is the phone *ringing* when I'm already talking on it?

MONSTER. ROOOAAARRR!!!

SANDRA. *(turning her head to fix him with a deadpan stare)* Oh "roar" yourself.

*(***GERALD**, *the show's director comes up to the stage from the back of house.* **JIM**, *a young stagehand emerges from backstage and props himself against the stage left door.)*

GERALD. Okay everybody…uh…obviously that *was* going great…right up until *the lightning went insane and…*

(The phone gives a long, persistent ring.)

(shouting towards the control booth) Phil! *Phil! Can we cut the bloody phone noise? Please?*

(Ringing stops.)

GERALD. *(cont.)* Thank you. Now. What happened?

PHIL. *(offstage) (calling back from the control booth)* Just a sec…

GERALD. No, Phil. *NOT* "just a sec." *Now! What in blazes just happened there?*

PHIL. *(offstage)* I don't know…a short in one of the dimmers maybe…

GERALD. Well, I can *see THAT*, Phil. What I want to know is *why? "Why"* when this is our last rehearsal are you doing this to me? *"Why"* do you insist on giving me reassurances that turn out to be…well, frankly… *untrue*, Phil? *"Why,"* in short, do you insist on *lying* to me…*Phil?* I *thought* you said you'd *fixed* that?

PHIL. *(offstage)* I thought I did.

GERALD. Well…you quite obviously *didn't, did you? Phil.*

PHIL. *(offstage)* I guess not… *(under his breath)* …you artsy-fartsy piece of –

GERALD. *"DID YOU…Phil?"*

PHIL. *(offstage)* NO!

GERALD. There now. Doesn't it feel better to have the truth – awful as it may be…*tiresome* as it may be… *ALTOGETHER BLOODY INCONVENIENT*…as it may be – doesn't it feel better to have it out in the open?

MONSTER. *(aside to* **SANDRA***)* Are we taking five, now?

SANDRA. *(aside to* **MONSTER***, in a sing-song voice) Not now!*

PHIL. *(offstage) (flatly, responding to* **GERALD***)* Yeah. Sure.

GERALD. *(to* **PHIL***)* Good! Then perhaps we have – through the auspices of this open-hearted and truthful dialogue – sown the very seeds which will blossom into the answer to my next question: *What the hell was going on with the phone? THAT*, at least, has been working up until now.

PHIL. *(offstage) (muttering again)* I was leaning on the button…

GERALD. Come again?

PHIL. *(offstage) (loud and sharp)* I was *leaning…on…the BUTTON!*

GERALD. Might I ask…*why?*

PHIL. *(offstage) (snapping)* Because it *felt good! OKAY!?!* Why do you think? I was reaching across it to try and fix the dimmer and I accidentally leaned on the phone-button. Alright!?! Sue me!

GERALD. I've been considering it… *(to his actors)* Sorry everyone!

MONSTER. Can we take five now?

(**SANDRA** *glares at him.*)

(oblivious) What?

GERALD. YES! We CAN take "five," it seems. In multiples of *TEN*, it seems…as we wait for Phil to *yet again* solve the mystery of lightning. *(to* **PHIL***)* Oh…and Phil…as long as we *have* come to a *grinding* halt…might I also note that the first thunder crash was *too loud* and the first lightning flash was far and away *too bright?*

PHIL. *(offstage)* Noted.

GERALD. …We *are* trying to waken in the audience a slow-building sense of primordial dread, after all. To slowly reintroduce those elemental fears that chill the marrow of the animal within us all: darkness; storms; isolation; and the incontrovertible fact of Time's merciless march towards that most *ultimate* unknown… *Death itself.*

PHIL. *(offstage)* Your point being?

GERALD. Subtlety, Philip, subtlety. A little less *Wagnerian*, if it's not too much to ask, Philip. A little less *sturm und drang,* next time if you please.

PHIL. *(offstage)* I hadn't preset the levels.

GERALD. *(lightly)* And why would you have? Eh? Why *would you!?!* This is, after all, only our last chance to *get this right!*

JIM. I thought the whispers were pretty creepy.

GERALD. I beg your pardon?

JIM. The whispers…at the top of the show…during the blackout. All those voices whispering. It was creepy. Especially the crying woman calling for her baby.

SANDRA. *(confused)* What? What voices? What whispering?

MONSTER. I didn't hear any whispering.

JIM. What are you talking about? It was almost louder than the thunder. You must have heard it.

GERALD. Philip!

PHIL. *(offstage)* What now!?!

GERALD. Our eager young gopher here claims that you took the liberty of introducing a new sound effect at the top of the show…apparently for his benefit only.

PHIL. *(offstage)* What sound effect?

GERALD. Whispers, Philip. A veritable chorus of them, apparently. *(beat)* Now, Philip…and be careful how you answer this…Is it the case that: A) Our young friend here is *insane? Or* B) That you are *unemployed?*

PHIL. *(offstage)* He's nuts. There's no whispering effects in the whole play.

GERALD. Well…let the angels sing his praises, Philip has *finally* delivered – unto we the undeserving – an answer I can actually *live with. (to* **JIM***)* You, my young friend, are insane. I don't ever want to hear from you again. Is that clear?

JIM. Well, I…

GERALD. *(wagging a cautioning finger)* Ah-ah-*ah!* I can *hear you…*

SANDRA. Oh…leave him alone. He was only trying to help.

GERALD. Et tu, Bruté?

SANDRA. *(ignoring him)* Is there anything you want us to work on while we're waiting?

GERALD. How about world peace?

SANDRA. I'll take that as a no. So I guess it's break time everybody.

JIM. Wait! Don't go anywhere. I want to you to have a look at some really neat things I found backstage.

SANDRA. Typical crew…Always trying to get us girls to look at your "things" backstage.

JIM. *(embarrassed)* Um…oh…I didn't mean…

SANDRA. *(gently mocking)* Oh *look!* He's *blushing!* That's so *sweet!* *(beat)* Alright…just for that I *will* look at your *thing.*

JIM. I'll be right back.

> *(Exit* JIM, *up left.)*

> *(The others wait in silence for a few beats.* SANDRA *sighs. Silence.* GERALD *coughs once. Silence.)*

MONSTER. I'm hungry.

> *(Enter* JIM, *up left, carrying a Ouija board and two placards.)*

JIM. Look at these! They were stuffed behind a loose panel of black pegboard.

SANDRA. What are they?

JIM. Here look!

> (JIM *holds up the first placard. Looking aged and a little faded, with a garish font suggestive of the second quarter of the 20th Century, it proclaims: The Powers Of Presto!)*

SANDRA. *(reading)* The Powers Of Presto!

GERALD. Ah…Alliteration and exclamation marks…the calling cards of the talentless.

MONSTER. Actually, he was really great.

GERALD. *(gasps in mock horror)* It speaks.

MONSTER. I remember seeing him perform here as a kid.

GERALD. He was a "child performer"?

MONSTER. No. When *I* was a kid.

GERALD. The Good Lord endowed us with syntax for a reason.

SANDRA. *(looking at* GERALD *but talking to* MONSTER*)* Go on, Hank.

MONSTER. He was one of those "mentalists." You know, a "psychic." He'd read peoples minds and hypnotize them and stuff. I don't remember much about it except that I loved it at the time.

SANDRA. *(to* JIM*)* What else have you got?

(JIM *shows the next placard which has simple clear, blockish letters, and reads: WKBS PRESENTS.)*

"Presents" what?

(JIM *shrugs.)*

MONSTER. "Prime Time Variety." *(mimics a radio announcer)* "Good Evening, Friends. And Welcome. I'm Corwin Haygood and do you know what? It's *Eight O'Clock!* It's *Saturday Night!* And that can only mean it's *Variety Time in Prime Time* right here on WKBS…"

GERALD. Hank! I didn't know you had it in you. How come you never have that much life onstage?

MONSTER. Because I'm supposed to be dead onstage.

SANDRA. *(laughing at* GERALD*)* Ha! Ha! Got you there didn't he Mister Smartypants?

MONSTER. Anyway, Corwin Haywood was the announcer for the show and it went somewhere different every week. It was always "coming to you live" from some theatre or other. They even did a broadcast from this place when Presto performed here. That's the night I saw him. *(beat)* I remember something really terrible happened that night…Now how can I *possibly* not remember what it was? I was *there.* Was it…Presto had a heart attack onstage maybe? Or…No. Huh. Can't remember.

JIM. Maybe he died while he was using… *THIS!*

(JIM *triumphantly presents the Ouija board he's holding. It looks old and worn and is stained with something dark over a good deal of its surface.)*

SANDRA. Oh my god!

MONSTER. He might've. I remember him using one of those.

GERALD. One of what? What is it?

SANDRA. *(taking the board from* **JIM***)* Oh my god! I *can't* believe it! I haven't seen one of these since I was a kid.

GERALD. Oh look! Here comes my echo, bouncing back to me from the distant canyon walls of your *disregard…* "One of what? What is it?"

SANDRA. It's a Wee-jee board. *(shows it to him)*

GERALD. Not unless they can't spell. It says "Oui-*ja*" *(pronounces the "j" in "ja")*

SANDRA. Well…if you want to get *picky*…it *should* be pronounced: Wee yah. It's made up of the French and German words for "Yes." But everybody always pronounces it "Wee-jee."

MONSTER. Why don't they just call it a "Yes-yes Board"?

SANDRA. Because they *don't.*

GERALD. How do you play it?

SANDRA. You don't "play" it. You *use* it…for communicating with the spirit world.

GERALD. Uh-huh.

SANDRA. No really. That's what you use it for. See? It has the letters of the alphabet, the numbers one through nine and zero as well, and the words "Yes" and "No." You ask it questions and the pointer spells out or points to the answer. And it really works too.

GERALD. Sure it does.

MONSTER. It does. I used one myself once. I didn't think it would work but it did. Scared the heck out of me, I can tell you that.

GERALD. Right.

JIM. How does it work?

SANDRA. You need a planchette.

JIM. A what?

SANDRA. A pointer. It's the thing everybody rests their fingertips on that moves around the board to spell out the answers to whatever we ask.

JIM. Oh. I didn't find one of those…

SANDRA. You can use anything as long as it'll slide on the board. A shot glass'll work.

JIM. Hey…there's one over here. *(heading offstage)* I think it's left over from the amateur theatre group that was in here last week.

(Exit JIM *to get the glass.)*

GERALD. Shot glass? Is that what you used when you were "a kid?" If so, I think you might have a problem.

(Enter JIM *with shot glass.)*

SANDRA. Har-dee-har-harr. *(to* MONSTER*)* We need a table and some chairs. *(looks at* GERALD*) Three* should do.

(MONSTER *and* JIM *get the chairs and table from the onstage set.)*

GERALD. Don't move the set!

SANDRA. We'll put it all back. Relax. Now… *(to* JIM*)* I just need you and Hank to –

MONSTER. Whoa whoa *WHOA!* Not *me! I'm* not touching that thing. I told you…those things scare the heck out of me.

SANDRA. Oh. Well. In that case… *(looks at* GERALD*)*

GERALD. What? *(gasps, feigned surprise)* Oh! You need *me* now, do you? Well, it won't work. I don't believe in any of this stuff.

SANDRA. That doesn't matter. Just put your index finger on it like this…very lightly. Hank, can you get a pencil and paper so you can write the down the questions and the answers we get?

(HANK *gets paper and pencil.)*

(All three place their fingers on the shot glass planchette.)

GERALD. Now what?

SANDRA. We ask it questions.

JIM. Like what?

SANDRA. Shhh! Just be quiet for a second. We have to call the spirit of the board first.

GERALD. I've got a few suggestions for what we could call it…

SANDRA. Quiet. Now… *(to the board)* Hello? Are there any spirits here who would like to talk to us today?…Hello? Are there any –

JIM. *(amazed)* HEY! It's moving!

(The shot glass begins to slide around in circles.)

SANDRA. It's supposed to.

GERALD. Which one of you's pushing it?

SANDRA. No one's pushing it. It moves on its own.

GERALD. Really…You're not pushing this?

SANDRA. You'd feel it if I was. Now…Shhh! Are there any spirits who would like –

(The point suddenly slides to "Yes.")

JIM. WOW! Did you *see* that? It went right to "yes"!

SANDRA. That means we've got one.

GERALD. One what? An otherworldly spirit with nothing better to do than wait around to answer questions from total strangers?

SANDRA. Shush! Okay. Now. Do you have a name?

(The shot glass pointer moves to "yes.")

JIM. Yes.

SANDRA. Will you tell us your name?

(Pointer moves to "no.")

GERALD. "No"? That's a little *evasive* isn't it?

SANDRA. *(shrugs)* Sometimes they're like that. Okay. I have another question: I want to know if this was Presto's board. *(to the board)* Who owned this board?

(The shot glass pointer begins to point to letters.)

SANDRA. *(cont.) (reading as glass points)* O-W-N-S. Owns?

   (Glass slides to "yes" then starts to circle again.)

JIM. "Yes"?

GERALD. *(interested in spite of himself)* It seems to be correcting you.

SANDRA. Let's ask it: Were you correcting me?

   (Pointer moves to "yes.")

   Yes. So the owner is still alive?

   (Pointer continues to circle.)

JIM. Why isn't it answering?

SANDRA. The question's probably too open.

GERALD. What's "open" about it. The guy's either alive or dead isn't he?

SANDRA. Not from the spirit's point of view. You find they don't like thinking of themselves as "dead." Try again. Let's see…Are you saying the person who originally owned this board still owns it?

   (Pointer moves to "yes.")

JIM. Yes.

SANDRA. Okay. And is this the board that was used by the Powers Of Presto?

   (Pointer points to "yes.")

JIM. Yes.

SANDRA. *(to the others)* Wow! Hey Hank! We've got a piece of your childhood here. This was "Presto's" board.

   (Pointer moves to "No.")

JIM. Wow! Did you see that? It moved right across to "No."

GERALD. Apparently it's correcting you again.

SANDRA. Are you saying Presto isn't or wasn't the owner of this board?

   (Pointer slides to "Yes.")

JIM. Yes.

SANDRA. Can you tell us who was?

(Pointer begins to spell.)

JIM. *(reading aloud)* M-R-L-N…What does that mean?

SANDRA. They sometimes leave letters out to talk faster. Most often vowels. It could be…*Merlin.*

GERALD. Merlin? Oh sure. Ask how the rest of the Knights of the Round Table are doing?

JIM. *(still reading)* B-L-C-K…

GERALD. That doesn't make any sense.

JIM. *(excited)* Actually, I think it *might.* I'll check it later. Wait…it's spelling something else…

SANDRA. *(reading)* M-Y-F-A-U-L-T…"My fault?" -M-Y-S-B-K-

GERALD. I think it's becoming illiterate.

SANDRA. SHHH!

MONSTER. Was that last thing "M-Y-S-B-K"?

GERALD. Oh! I've got one! *(with a look at the booth)* How does Philip die?

SANDRA. *(appalled)* Don't ask questions like that!

GERALD. I was just want to know if I'm the one who does it!

JIM. It's answering… *(reading)* …I-R-E-F-I-R-E..

MONSTER. Fire?

JIM. …I don't know. It's still going…-W-I-R-E…

SANDRA. Wire?

JIM. S-A-D-Y-T-O-O

SANDRA. NO!

(She shoves the shot glass and board away from her.)

JIM. What? What?

GERALD. Sandra! Take it easy!

SANDRA. I don't want to know!

GERALD. Know what? What are you talking about?

SANDRA. It *was* answering your question…but not *just* about Philip. It was trying to say I – *(breaks off, upset)*

GERALD. No it wasn't! It spelled "Sady" not "Sandy." And nobody's *ever* called you "Sandy."

SANDRA. *(shaking her head in denial)* No, Gerald. You don't understand…that's what my Grandfather used to call me. "Sady." Not "Sandy"…"Sady." Nobody knows that. Nobody else *ever* knew that…

GERALD. And *neither did the board*. It *can't* "know" anything. It's just a cheap piece of cardboard.

JIM. *(thoughtful)* I don't know… *(snaps his fingers)* Right! I wanted to check that.

(Exit **JIM**, *running out through the house to the lobby.)*

GERALD. *(takes her by the arms)* Look, Sandra…I can't *afford* to have you getting all upset over this. This is our *dress rehearsal.* If I'd known this stupid little parlour-trick game had that much power over you I never would have let you touch it. Now…are you going to be alright? Are you? I want you to call up all of your professionalism, personal force of will and *not* inconsiderable acting talents…so that you can look me in the eye and tell me you're going to be alright.

SANDRA. *(deliberately smiles and looks him in the eye)* I'll be fine. Sorry. Hank was right. Should've remembered how those things can shake you up.

GERALD. Those *things* don't *do anything.* I don't know exactly *how* it works but I'm sure we must be willing it to move somehow…at some subconscious level maybe even if we don't know it.

(Enter **JIM** *at the back of the house flipping through a book.)*

JIM. *(calling)* I found it! It's right here!

GERALD. What? What are you going on about?

*(***JIM** *gets up onstage still looking at the book.)*

JIM. Hey, Hank…What'd the board say the second time Miss Roberts asked it who its owner was?

MONSTER. *(checking his notes)* It spelled out M-R-L-N-B-L-C-K.

JIM. Right. And we thought M-R-L-N was "Merlin," right?

GERALD. I was joking.

JIM. Well, yeah, about the Round Table and all that but if B-L-C-K stands for "Black"… *(flipping pages)* Listen to this… This is from "Our Stage In History" by Thomas Fox. It's a local history book. I was looking at it on break the other day. The theatre owner bought one because it's a complete history of all the theaters that have ever existed in this area and pretty much every-thing that's known about them: what was performed; who was in it; and there was this whole section…on… *(flipping pages)*

GERALD. If you don't mind I'd prefer we just forgot about this whole business…

JIM. *Here it is! (reading)* Merlin Black – Born: Thomas Merlin Black, March 24th 1874. Died: October 31st, 1926. A Master of both Stage and Slight of Hand Magic, Black was a self-described "Mesmerist, Conjurer, Escape Artist, and Master of the Occult Arts." *(skipping down the page)* He performed…this stage…more than 100 times…Oh! Here…On October 31st, 1926, his body was discovered in the basement of the Orpheus Theatre……even though, his scheduled appearance at the Orpheus on that date – purportedly to be his "Farewell Performance" – had been canceled almost a month beforehand. Black was found sprawled across the Ouija board which had become an object of great importance in his life both on and offstage, dead of an apparent suicide resulting from his occult beliefs. A handwritten note was found clutched in one fist. It is reproduced below…" *(searching)* …Okay. Here: *(reads)* "The blood of four into the board. / The First one through reaps the reward. / The second must therein remain, / To feed the First with meat of pain. / To the whisper'd call of the First, / childless mother…Death's chains to burst./ Thus freed the First in spirit waits/ 'Til recall'd by Unbeliever's blood…back through the parting gate."

GERALD. Well…if he was trying to make his living as a poet, it's small wonder he killed himself.

MONSTER. *(snapping his fingers)* RIGHT! That's it! I REMEM-BER now! Merlin Black…*that* was the guy Presto was trying to get in touch with using the Ouija board. That was when all hell broke loose. I –

PHIL. Okay. We're ready to go.

GERALD. Saved by the bell. Okay everyone…let's put all this back where it belongs!

(The others put things back where they got them.)

PHIL. Sorry for the delay. There was a short in the wiring. I think Ben Franklin put this rig together himself.

GERALD. Well –

JIM. Hey…did he say "wire"?

GERALD. Did you know you're three seconds away from the bread-line?

JIM. *(holding up the placards)* Is it okay if I keep these?

GERALD. One…two…

JIM. I'll take that as a "yes-as-long-as-I'm-quick-about-it."

GERALD. Alright, Philip…everyone! Let's get the curtain closed and take it once more from the top. Oh…and Philip…I don't want *any* ghostly whispers to be heard by *anyone* this time.

*(Exit **GERALD** as the curtains close. **JIM** remains in front of the curtain looking at his prized "finds.")*

JIM. Welcome to my collection boys. You're coming home with me.

(He sets them out of the way as far down left in front of the curtain as possible and turns to go backstage. He stops and turns back, considering. He picks up the Ouija Board and looks at it.)

On second thought…*you* can stay here.

*(Exit **JIM** through the curtains with the Ouija Board.)*

Scene Two

"PRESTO"

(Enter **CORWIN HAYGOOD***, radio show host with an old-fashioned stand-up microphone – an enunciator – extreme down right, in front of the curtain, and a* **CIGARETTE GIRL** *extreme down left carrying an easel and three placards. Two of these placards are the brand new "originals" of the ones Jim found backstage in Scene One. The third is an "APPLAUSE" sign. While* **CORWIN** *speaks, the* **CIGARETTE GIRL** *sets the easel in place, puts the applause sign on the floor covering the placards left behind from Scene One, and sets remaining two placards on the easel. First she places the one that reads "WKBS PRESENTS" – making sure the audience see it clearly – and then, in front of it she sets the one that reads "The POWERS of Presto!")*

CORWIN HAYGOOD. *(to the audience)* Okay folks. Our break to the studio will be over in just a few seconds. We hope you're enjoying the show so far… *(waits for some applause to start, then cups a hand to one ear, leaning forward)* I *say: I hope you're enjoying the show so far…!*

(CIGARETTE GIRL *holds up APPLAUSE sign, incites the audience to applaud.)*

(taking his cue from someone unseen, offstage) That's great. Well, we're almost back so if you could help us out with a nice round of *really enthusiastic applause* in 3…2…

(CIGARETTE GIRL *holds up APPLAUSE sign, again inciting the audience as needed.)*

"Good Evening, Friends. And Welcome back To *Prime Time Variety* on WKBS…"

(CIGARETTE GIRL *gestures to end the applause.)*

CORWIN HAYGOOD. *(cont.)* …brought to you by your good friends at *Silver Fox! Silver Fox,* fast-becoming everybody's favourite smoke. I am still your host, Corwin Haygood and we are *still* coming to you live from the beautiful Orpheus Theatre, where *Presto,* the Master Magician, Hypnotist, and Spiritualist…

(**CIGARETTE GIRL** *raises the APPLAUSE sign as the curtain opens to reveal,* **PRESTO** *and his assistant* **LUCRECIA** *center stage. There is a high, pedestal table with an Ouija board on it down left of center.*)

…Has been dazzling the audience with feats of knowledge skill and magic. Already, we have witnessed as he identified the secret word written on a card and sealed in an envelope by yours truly…and believe me folks, I didn't let anyone sneak a peek. We watched him take less than 10 seconds to find a pocket watch given to a random member of our live audience and concealed upon their person. We have witnessed a fascinating demonstration of the powers of suggestion using only members of our studio audience and then…just before that last word from our sponsor, Presto took questions from the audience offering to help any and all comers, whatever their problem. Among these was a gentleman who was informed by Presto *not* to drive home tonight without checking the brakes on his car *and* the delightful wife of our very own Mayor. She had apparently lost one of her most prized pieces of jewelry: one of a pair of *sapphire* earrings given to her dear, departed mother as a gift by no less a notable than Charles Dickens himself, perhaps the greatest man of letters of the 19th century. She was wondering if Presto could help her find them. And if you don't mind, Maestro…would you please repeat the reply you gave for the benefit of our listening audience?

PRESTO. Not at all, Corwin. I told the lovely Lady Bernice that she should look behind the mahogany dresser in her boudoir, that she would find them there, along with her favourite red silk scarf which she had as yet to realize was also missing.

(**CIGARETTE GIRL** *raises APPLAUSE sign.*)

CORWIN HAYGOOD. *(to the audience)* Isn't that incredible folks? Isn't it just? Now, unfortunately, much as she hated to leave this fine entertainment behind, the First Lady of our fair "town" did have to leave during our last break. It *was,* however, so that she could attend a fund-raiser to help needy children the world over, so I trust Presto won't take it personally. *(a look to* **PRESTO***)*

PRESTO. No. No, of course not. Her excuse is as understandable as it is selfless and laudable.

CORWIN HAYGOOD. I could not have said it better myself, but ummm…you know, Maestro…

PRESTO. Yes?

CORWIN HAYGOOD. The good lady *did* have time to make a quick phone call from the lobby before departing.

PRESTO. *(smug)* She did?

CORWIN HAYGOOD. Yes. She did. And she was able to get her maid, Cora, to go and have a look behind that dresser in her boudoir…

PRESTO. She did?

CORWIN HAYGOOD. Yes. She did.

PRESTO. Well, then I am sure she is very relieved.

CORWIN HAYGOOD. I haven't told you what Cora found… *or didn't find,* yet.

PRESTO. *(fully confident)* Oh, I know what she found.

CORWIN HAYGOOD. Are you *sure* you know?

PRESTO. Absolutely.

CORWIN HAYGOOD. *(to the audience)* Well…that confidence would seem almost unshakable, Maestro. *(pulls a piece of paper from his pocket)* Now, obviously there wasn't a lot of time and the lady was in some haste but she *insisted* I read this to you and apologize for it's brevity. So here it is, in the lady's own hand: Dear Presto… *(shouting)* THANK YOU FOR HELPING ME RECOVER MY LOST EARRING!

(**CIGARETTE GIRL** *holds up APPLAUSE sign.* **CORWIN** *encourages the applause and lets it continue a few moments before gesturing for quiet again.*)

CORWIN HAYGOOD. *(cont.)* That's right, Presto. The earring was *exactly* where you'd said it would be. It was on the floor, behind the dresser in her boudoir, hooked onto a red silk scarf that must've dragged it along when it slipped down behind the dresser!

PRESTO. As I knew it would be.

CORWIN HAYGOOD. You never had a doubt?

PRESTO. No.

CORWIN HAYGOOD. Not even for a moment?

PRESTO. No.

CORWIN HAYGOOD. Well then, I suppose it will also come as no surprise to you when I tell you that Jack, the gentleman you spoke to in our audience earlier, went out and had a little look at his car and discovered that his brakes *were indeed on the absolute verge of giving out.*

(**CIGARETTE GIRL** *raises APPLAUSE sign.*)

(*after a few beats, quiets applause again*) You're not surprised at all are you?

PRESTO. No. I cannot say that I am.

CORWIN HAYGOOD. Well, alright Maestro. You've got me convinced. And I think most if not all of our audience here convinced as well. And if the folks at home aren't amazed, that's our fault not yours.

PRESTO. Thank you. You are very kind.

CORWIN HAYGOOD. So tell us, Presto. What have you got cooked up for us in this last segment.

PRESTO. Ah, my good friend Corwin, audience members and delightful guests who are listening in on us from afar…On this night, this most mystic and *magical* night of the year, October 31st…I hope to achieve, in your presence and with your help, something that has *never been attempted before.* But to understand the nature of this feat, I must first explain what has gone before. So, with your indulgence…

CORWIN HAYGOOD. By all means, Maestro. Ladies and gentlemen, in the theatre and in our listening audience, I leave you in the capable hands of...*Presto!*

PRESTO. Thank you, Corwin. Ladies and gentlemen, I tell you now the story of one of the *greatest* and most *mysterious practitioners of my profession.* He was born on March 24th, 1874 and died on October 31st, nineteen hundred and twenty-six. But wait! For those among you who recognize those dates as the ones that mark the beginning and end of the life of Harry Houdini, I must tell you that though you are correct in this, the conclusion you have likely drawn is wrong. For *MERLIN BLACK,* perhaps the greatest of us all, though by no means the *most* famous, is the man to whom those dates pertain. Merlin Black, who died on this *very night, All Hallows Eve,* in 1926. Merlin Black, whose true face, ever-painted with a grim mask of grease-paint, was *never seen* by his adoring public, nor by – so far as is known – anyone else who ever knew him. There exist *no images, drawings, or photographs* of him that do not depict his theatrical alter ego, a character he always referred to quite simply as...*the Juggler.*

(With a gesture, **PRESTO** *sends his assistant* **LUCRECIA** *to stand by the table with the Ouija board on it.)*

And although juggling was just one of the many skills of this art that he had mastered even as a youth...it was not juggling, or fire-swallowing, or escape, or slight-of-hand, or stage-illusion, or any of the *other* skills he had mastered that held fascination for *the Juggler* even unto the day of his death. Only this...

*(***PRESTO** *gestures towards* **LUCRECIA** *who holds up the Ouija board.)*

...The Ouija. The "yes-yes" board. The *talking wood.* Or to some – to those whose study of the arcane arts extend well beyond conceiving parlor tricks to delight the public...to those who truly wear the mantle *Magician... (indicates the board)* – *The Conduit.* It was only *this* that the Juggler felt he had yet to master. It was in his mind, the means to communicate with that other world, the one beyond the grave and even…perhaps…a gateway through which the soul might pass towards *death*…or through which the soul might *return to LIFE!*

(PRESTO *nods to* **LUCRECIA** *who sets the board down again.)*

PRESTO. *(cont.)* Now almost as much has been made of Merlin Black, the Juggler's obsession with death as has been made of the significant connection between himself and the Great Houdini: Born the same day; Died the same day. And indeed, this too proved a connection between them. For while the Great Houdini – offended as he was by *false* spiritualists and mediums who could not help him communicate with his departed mother – made it his life's work to debunk and dismiss those who claimed the ability to communicate *beyond the veil of Death…the Juggler, Merlin Black* made it his own life's work to prove Houdini wrong.

(PRESTO *paces as he addresses the audience.)*

Like the great author of the Sherlock Holmes stories, Sir Arthur Conan Doyle – with whom both he and Houdini had many dealings – Black felt that communication with the dead was not only possible but that the keys to achieving it have been found and lost many times in human history. Houdini and he argued the matter many times in correspondence. But when Houdini publicly ridiculed Black's beliefs during one of his performances for a certain Head of State, he gained for himself an enemy in *the Juggler.* In fact, there is one story – a brief one, I promise – that suggests the Juggler might even have been responsible for the Great Houdini's death. As most of you will know, Houdini suffered the terrible injury that ultimately proved fatal while backstage at a performance in Montreal in the fall of 1926. A student of McGill University, hoping to win Houdini's standing challenge that no man alive, no matter how strong, could knock the wind out of him with a single punch to the stomach. Those who did try all agree that Houdini's stomach was no more yielding to a fist than an iron door two inches thick. This was not magic. It was simply a tribute to the incredible strength of Houdini's abdominal muscles. But…on this one occasion, Houdini, apparently distracted, was caught by the blow unawares and suffered a great hurt. A hurt that would shortly thereafter rob him of the strength he needed to perform his greatest escape in that tragic incident that led to his final demise in Detroit.

(**PRESTO** *lowers his head and puts his hand over his heart for a moment.*)

PRESTO. *(cont.)* The story claims that Houdini was reading a telegram sent to him by Merlin Black the moment before he was punched and that it was *that message* that so distracted him he did not hear the *bruiser's* challenge. A backstage worker claimed he retrieved that telegram and though he never produced it in evidence, claiming it was later stolen from him, he swore to his dying day that the message read: "There is another side. Stop. You'll see. Stop. And I'll be there to show you around. Stop. Happy Halloween. Stop. Signed, the Juggler." As I say, that is only a story and I have never seen evidence to support it. Something that is a matter of record though, is the fact that Merlin Black killed himself in the first instants of October 31, 1926 in the basement of *this very theatre.*

(*He gestures to* **LUCRECIA,** *who holds up the board once more to show the stain.*)

That stain you see was made by the very blood of Merlin Black when he died by his own hand over that very board, without explanation. And I have told you all this because I intend to attempt, on this very night, to contact Merlin Black, the Juggler, on the anniversary of his death, *using his own Ouija board,* in the hopes of finding out what happened that final fateful night. (*smiles, joking to lighten the mood*) And perhaps, if he knows how we might get in contact with Houdini. (*looks to* **CORWIN**) With your permission?

CORWIN HAYGOOD. By all means, Maestro. *(for his listeners)* Presto is now moving into the audience to select his volunteers. Please stand by…

PRESTO. *(pointing to a man in the audience)* Pardon me, sir, could you tell me your name please.

ROGER. Roger Everett.

PRESTO. Roger Everett. Would you come up to the stage please, sir?

> *(**ROGER** leaves his seat and heads up to the stage, where **LUCRECIA** gets him to stand by the table with the Ouija board.)*

> *(pointing out a woman in the audience)* And yourself, Madame? Yes Madam, the lovely lady in the beautiful blue dress. Might I ask your name?

> *(**EVELYN** bursts into a high-pitched and amusingly distinctive fit of embarrassed, giggling laughter.)*

> Would you care to join us on the stage, please Madame?

> *(With another fit of excited laughter, **EVELYN** heads for the stage, bringing her purse with her. Where **LUCRECIA** will place her by the table as well.)*

> And now, just one more…perhaps you sir? What is your name.

TOM. Tom.

PRESTO. Tom. Would you please join us, Tom?

TOM. I don't think you want me up there.

PRESTO. And why would that be, sir?

TOM. I don't believe in any of this guff.

PRESTO. *(laughs)* Ah! But how perfect! We have a Doubting Thomas! *(to **TOM**)* Please sir, come up to the stage. We shall be all the better off if we are successful for having at least one *avowed disbeliever* in our midst. *(crossing to the table)* Now, my lady with the charming laugh, may we know your name?

EVELYN. *(through more giggles)* Evie…*EVELYN!* It's Evelyn. Most people just call me Evie.

PRESTO. Well, which do you prefer?

EVELYN. *(more giggles)* Evie.

PRESTO. Evie, I am honoured to meet you and thank you for your assistance.

(**PRESTO** *kisses her hand, and she bursts into another fit of giggles.)*

And now, Roger. Might we know a little about you, Roger? Your occupation, for example?

ROGER. I am a theatre-owner.

PRESTO. A theatre-owner? *(to the audience)* I swear we've never met before.

ROGER. *(to the audience)* He's telling the truth. We haven't.

PRESTO. Well, a theatre-owner. What a co-incidence! Not this theatre I hope?

ROGER. Not anymore. I sold it a few years ago. I'm just here as a patron tonight.

PRESTO. Well, we're very glad you came, Roger. *(to* **TOM***)* And now, Tom. Is it Tom? Or Thomas?

TOM. I prefer Tom.

PRESTO. Then Tom it is. And what do you do Tom?

TOM. I thought you were a psychic.

PRESTO. *(laughs)* And so I am, Tom. But it *is* customary to ask, for the sake of politeness. However, as you are an honest unbeliever, would you like me to answer my own question?

TOM. *(shrugs)* If you think you can.

PRESTO. I suppose, for the benefit of our audience I should confirm that to the best of your knowledge we have never met before this?

TOM. Definitely not. I'd remember your outfit.

PRESTO. *(laughs)* Well if we *haven't* met before, this must not be *your watch.* *(holds up a watch)* I wonder whose it might be?

(**TOM** *searches for his watch but doesn't find it. He is truly taken aback.)*

TOM. Um…uh…that *is* mine.

CORWIN HAYGOOD. *(chuckling, into the microphone)* For the benefit of our listeners, Presto has just produced a complete stranger's watch from his own pocket and I swear as I live and breath he *never* came within five feet of the man.

TOM. That's…my watch.

*(***ROGER*** bursts out laughing.)*

PRESTO. Of course, it is, Tom. And you'll want to keep hold of that. As the plant foreman for a major manufacturer of automobiles it's your job to keep track of production, schedules…coffee breaks is it not?

*(***TOM*** nods.)*

Of course, it is. *(joking)* Unfortunately, I cannot declare the name of the manufacturer because I have no idea if they advertise with this station. *(chuckles and holds out Tom's watch.)* But I have no doubt you will be wanting your watch returned…

*(***TOM*** takes the watch.)*

Oh! And you'll be wanting this as well… *(produces Tom's billfold from his own jacket pocket.)*

TOM. *(realizing his own wallet's gone even as he reaches for it.)* How did you – ? *(Takes the wallet and looks through it, nodding. Holds it up and looking at ***CORWIN***.)* It's my billfold, too!

CORWIN HAYGOOD. Presto has also returned Tom's billfold. But Tom! Is it still folding any bills?

PRESTO. Well, of course, there *is a finder's fee*…No! I am just joking. It's all there. You can count it. Ten dollars and forty-three cents.

*(***ROGER*** is still laughing.)*

Roger…you'll be wanting your keys…

*(***ROGER***'s eyes go wide as saucers and he howls even harder.)*

And *your* billfold. *(hands them to ***ROGER***)* I won't say how much is in it in case you have to walk past any dark alleyways on the way home.

ROGER. I can't *believe it!*

PRESTO. Oh! There is one more thing. *(produces a white envelope which he hands to* **ROGER***)*

CORWIN HAYGOOD. Presto is giving Roger a white envelope.

ROGER. This isn't mine.

PRESTO. No. But I believe *this is? (produces a folding knife and opens it)*

ROGER. *(pointing at the knife)* Alright, now *that's…that's…*

PRESTO. That's what you'll need to open the envelope, Roger or we're going to run out of time.

(Laughing, **ROGER** *takes the knife and cuts the envelope open.)*

CORWIN HAYGOOD. For our listeners: Presto just gave Roger an envelope to open and then presented Roger with *Roger's own* knife so he could open it.

*(***ROGER** *sets the knife and opened envelope down on the table so he can remove the folded piece of paper within.)*

ROGER. *(to himself)* I can't believe this. I *cannot* believe this…

(He opens the piece of paper, reads, and bursts out laughing.)

CORWIN HAYGOOD. Roger is laughing at something written on a piece of paper within the envelope. Roger! What does it say?

ROGER. *(holding the paper up)* It says…"Believe it!"

EVELYN. You *don't say!*

TOM. Wow.

ROGER. *(Something on the back side of the sheet catches his eye ,and he gasps.)* Oh my LORD!

CORWIN HAYGOOD. What is it, Roger.

ROGER. On the other side of the sheet it says: "Yes, Evelyn…I *do* say!" And below that it says, "Coming from you Tom, 'Wow' is high praise indeed.

(**CIGARETTE GIRL** *raises the APPLAUSE sign and all the people on stage burst into enthusiastic applause which, after a moment,* **PRESTO** *quells with a gesture.*)

PRESTO. NOW! *(claps his hands together once)* Enough frivolity. Down to business. I would like the three of you to place your hands upon the planchette, very lightly. And just concentrate on relaxing, breathing slowly in and out.

(They all comply. **EVIE** *giggles then calms herself.)*

And while they are calming themselves, settling down and relaxing, I will explain for the benefit of our listening audience that the Ouija board is a rectangular board approximately one foot long and two and a half feet wide. The size is not important, I just mention it to convey a picture. It is usually made of wood but it may be made of almost any flat, smooth material. Upon its surface are printed all the letters of the alphabet, the words Yes and No, a sun and a moon and the numbers zero and one through nine. Our guests are resting their fingers on the *planchette,* which is a flat piece of wood cut roughly into a Valentine shape. Again, the shape is unimportant so long as there is an agreed-upon part of the *planchette* that serves as a pointer. For that is what it is. And when, as I hope shall happen tonight, one is conversing with the spirits through the board, the *planchette* will move across the board and point to the symbols, letters, and numbers in order to spell out their responses. Though I should point out that sometimes in their haste, the spirits spelling may become somewhat…"creative" shall we say? This is all clear? Good. Then we begin. *(walking around the three at the table)* Remaining calm. Relaxing. Breathing. Fingers resting very lightly on the *planchette. Remember* you need not push or pull the *planchette.* It will move on its own with no help from you save your open minds.

(Having completely circled them, **PRESTO** *stands center of the table.* **ROGER** *is nearest to him.* **TOM** *is on the upstage side of the table, and* **EVIE** *is on the stage left side.)*

PRESTO. *(cont.) (to the audience)* I must now ask for your *complete* silence please. I ask the spirits, spirits that may inhabit this place at this time to talk to us. We are hoping to learn something of our departed friend Merlin Black. I call on you spirits to make yourselves known to us through the answer board my three friends surround. Are there any spirits here who are willing to talk to us? Any spirits willing to talk to us?

(The planchette begins to slide in gentle circles around the board.)

EVELYN. *(gasps)* It's *moving.*

ROGER. Oh my – It *is moving.*

TOM. You're pushing it.

ROGER. Not me. It's moving *towards me.* Are *you* pushing it?

TOM. No. I'm not. I'm really not. This is…weird.

PRESTO. This is good! But please, my friends, remain as calm and relaxed as you can. Keep your fingers as lightly on the planchette as possible without breaking contact and again, *do not* try to anticipate or hinder its movements. *(beat)* Now…We know you are here…Will you talk to us?

(The planchette points to Yes then resumes circling.)

ROGER. Do you believe that?

EVELYN. It pointed to yes.

TOM. I don't believe it. I *saw* it but I don't believe it.

PRESTO. *(excited)* So you will talk to us? Tom will you be spokesman for the answers we get.

(Planchette points to Yes again.)

TOM. Sure. It just pointed to Yes again.

PRESTO. Will you tell us your name?

(Planchette points to No.)

TOM. No.

PRESTO. *(to the audience)* This is common, though no one knows why. Tell us spirit…if you won't tell us your name, what should we call you?

(Planchette begins to spell.)

TOM. *(as it spells)* J-U-G-G-L-E

PRESTO. Juggler?

TOM. V-Y-E-V-Y

ROGER. I think it's talking to you Evie.

PRESTO. Do you want us to call you Juggler?

(Planchette moves to No.)

TOM. No.

PRESTO. Do you want us to call you Evy?

EVELYN. I don't like that. It gives me the creeps.

(Planchette begins to spell, cycling through the letters faster and faster.)

TOM. E-V-Y-E-V-Y-E-V-Y

PRESTO. So we shall call you Evy. Do you know our friend, Merlin Black?

(Planchette spells, moving more aggressively around the board.)

TOM. H-A-H-A-H-A-

ROGER. "Ha ha ha"? What's so funny?

TOM. -H-A-P-Y-H-A-L-L-O

ROGER. "Happy Halloween?"

TOM. -T-T-Y-L-O-T-T-Y *(continues to spell "lotty" over the next couple lines of dialogue.)*

ROGER. "Lotty"? What does "Lotty" mean? Does anybody know what "Lotty" means.

*(**EVELYN** is now staring at the board, horrified. She begins to shake her head in denial.)*

EVELYN. Oh no…no…I don't like this…

TOM. -T-T-Y-H-E-L-P-H-E-L-P-M

CORWIN HAYGOOD. Now the board is spelling the words "lotty" and "help"…

EVELYN. *(becoming visibly upset)* No…*please*…

TOM. -M-A-M-A-M-A

ROGER. Mama?

EVELYN. *(starting to cry) Please don't do this…*

PRESTO. Spirit will you answer our questions about Merlin Black? If you will not we will call another.

TOM. -C-O-L-D-A-R-K-C-O-L-D-A-R-K

EVELYN. *(talking to the board) Why are you doing this? Stop it! Please!*

ROGER. "Cold ARK"? Or does it mean "Cold" *and* "Dark"

PRESTO. Spirit answer my questions or begone!

TOM. -W-E-L-L-W-E-L-L-M-A-M-A-M-A-

ROGER. We're back to "Mama" again.

EVELYN. *NO! NO! STOP IT! STOP IT! STOP SAYING THAT! It was an accident! It was an accident…*

TOM. *(suddenly looking at* **EVELYN** *and speaking in a child-like voice)* But it *wasn't an accident, Mama. You killed me!*

EVELYN. *(screams and backs away from the board)* NOOOOOOO!

(**TOM** *grabs her by one arm.*)

TOM. *You killed me, Mama! I fell down the well. You didn't save me!*

PRESTO. STOP IT, SPIRIT! I command you!

TOM. *Why didn't you save me, Mama? I called and called and called but you never came…*

(**EVELYN** *screams and tries to free herself but* **TOM** *won't let go.*)

It was cold in the water, Mama!

EVELYN. *NOOOO! PLEASE GOD NO!*

TOM. *Cold and dark…sooo dark…I'm escared of the dark Mama! (screams)* WHY DIDN'T YOU SAVE ME FROM THE DARK! YOU KILLED ME! YOU KILLED ME!

(**ROGER** *grabs hold of* **TOM**.)

ROGER. Tom! Let her go!

(**TOM** *grabs* **ROGER** *by the back of the neck and with apparently little effort slams* **ROGER***'s face down onto the table.* **ROGER** *shouts in pain and rises up, his upper lip and nose covered in blood.*)

ROGER. *(cont.) (clutching his face)* My nose! My – *(His eyes grow wide with panic, and he gasps, clutching at his left arm with his bloodied right hand.)*

PRESTO. *SPIRIT I COMMAND YOU TO LEAVE THIS PLACE! I COMMAND –*

TOM. *(in a different, sinister, almost demonic voice) YOU COMMAND NOTHING! YOU HAVE NO POWER! THE EYE DOESN'T LOOK ON YOU! (turns only his head to regard* **ROGER***)*

ROGER. *(gasping)* Oh my god…I'm…

*(***ROGER*** falls heavily against the table, trying to keep himself upright. Behind him* **TOM** *picks up the knife. He leans close by* **ROGER***'s ear as he reaches around and puts the knife to his throat.)*

TOM. *I TOLD YOU WHAT YOU'D GET FOR CANCELING MY LAST SHOW, EVERETT!*

ROGER. *(panicked even through his agony)* Black…

TOM. *JUGGLER! DID YOU THINK YOU COULD STOP ME?*

ROGER. *(weakening)* Black…

TOM. *YOU STOPPED NOTHING. AND NOW YOU WILL FEED ME!*

ROGER. …black… *(His eyes start rolling up in their sockets.)*

TOM. Juggler… *(leans closer)* …Jug-gler…Jug-u-lar…

*(***TOM*** cuts* **ROGER***'s throat. There is a lot of blood. He releases* **ROGER***, who gurgles wetly and falls.* **PRESTO** *and* **CORWIN** *rush him and struggle to get the knife from him.* **TOM** *goes still in their clutches. He turns his head to regard* **EVELYN***, who is backing away down left, horrified. He resumes speaking in his "child" voice.)*

It's cold and dark, Mama. Cold and dark.

EVELYN. No. OH GOD PLEASE NO! DON'T SAY THAT! DON'T TALK LIKE THAT!

TOM. *You'll know the cold and dark, too Mama. You'll know what it was like…*

*(***EVELYN*** screams and turns away, covering her ears.)*

CORWIN HAYGOOD. *Stop it! For God's Sake Stop it!*

TOM. *(back to his "Juggler" voice, looking at* **CORWIN***)* God? God can't help you, Haygood! You die here, Haygood! And there's nothing *God* can do about it! *You DIE HERE! IN THIS PLACE!*

CORWIN HAYGOOD. So what? I'm an *actor*, buddy. I'll die in lots of places worse than this!

TOM. *This is where you die! And I'll be watching!*

CORWIN HAYGOOD. Yeah? Well…it's always nice to have an audience…Now, *whatever you are…let Tom go.*

TOM. *I was done with this body anyway.*

*(***TOM'***s eyes roll up and he faints into their arms. They drag him center and lay him out. ***CORWIN*** slides the knife away across the floor towards the table.)*

(As **PRESTO** *moves to check on* **ROGER** *the lights begin to fade everywhere except on* **EVELYN** *who has backed away extreme down left.)*

PRESTO. *(to the audience) HE'S ALIVE! HE'S ALIVE! SOMEONE GET A DOCTOR! QUICKLY!*

(Only **EVELYN** *is lit now, and all onstage activity freezes. Her sobs begin to soften, and slowly she uncovers her head and raises her eyes, which have taken on a disconnected slightly insane glaze. She looks around as though newly arrived to this place. She looks at the frozen figures in darkness on the stage. Then turns away from them again. The* **CIGARETTE GIRL** *steps forward to comfort her, puts a hand on her shoulder.)*

CIGARETTE GIRL. It's alright, now, honey. It's going to be alright.

EVELYN. This is a frozen moment.

CIGARETTE GIRL. What?

EVELYN. *This*…it's a frozen moment. Like in the dream. Frozen moments only happen in dreams…don't they? Maybe this is a dream…

CIGARETTE GIRL. More of a nightmare, I'd say, honey.

EVELYN. You see that's where I was when it – I was dreaming, you see, when it – *(For a moment she is still, like a puppet whose strings have been cut, her eyes dull. Then suddenly, and with great animation…)* DID I EVER SHOW YOU THAT PICTURE OF MY DAUGHTER? *(grabs her purse)* I know it's in here somewhere. I always have it. I *never* leave it. I *never leave it…*Here it is! There she is. That's Charlotte. So beautiful. Like my mother.

*(***EVELYN*** *shows the picture to the* **CIGARETTE GIRL***, who reaches for it.)*

CIGARETTE GIRL. She's *very pretty…*

EVELYN. *NO! YOU CAN'T HAVE IT! (pulls the picture back and stares at it)* It's all I have of her now.

CIGARETTE GIRL. Is she…*gone?*

EVELYN. Yes. It was an accident. I was dreaming you see. *(remembering, enraptured)* Oh such a *beautiful dream!* It was beautiful. *I* was beautiful and I was at a party and there were Hollywood stars everywhere…Lionel Barrymore and Frederic March and *Valentino – he's still very attractive you know –* And there was that *very handsome newcomer,* Clark…somebody…

CIGARETTE GIRL. Gable?

EVELYN. *YES! That's him!* And I was being witty and charming and *everyone was hanging on my every word… (a change, becoming agitated)* Of course, Charlotte came into the room and started complaining she'd fallen in a puddle or something – children are always getting into their little *scrapes* at the worst time, don't you find? – So I told her it was alright and she could go back out and play. *(suddenly uncertain)* Maybe I should have gone over to her. I don't know. She seemed fine. A little wet was all. And after all…Errol Flynn and Douglas Fairbanks Jr. *were* offering to *fight a duel for my hand! (laughs fondly, remembering)* I, of course, was very nonchalant about the whole thing but *inside* I was *thrilled. (suddenly annoyed again)* But then…there she was *again!* With her "Mama! Mama! MAMA!" and her filthy, wet clothes dripping all over my new carpet and SPOILING EVERYTHING –

(She grabs **CIGARETTE GIRL***, pleading.)*

EVELYN. *(cont.) It wasn't my fault you see…*It was just that… *No matter how I tried to hush the child up, she wouldn't stop calling me. She just kept calling me and calling me…and she was RUINING VALENTINO's story with her interruptions so I told her to be quiet, Be Quiet, BE QUIET! WHY WON'T YOU BE QUIET!?!*

(She catches herself screaming and calms herself.)

That's when I had the frozen moment. Everyone, everything at the party stopped. They were all staring at Charlotte and they were all just…frozen. So I turned to her…and that was when I saw…she wasn't standing on the rug at all. No. She was up to her chest in water and her pretty pink dress was all soiled and floating up around her and the ribbons in her hair – the little bows at the front – they were all torn and soaked in blood because she'd hit her head. And that was when I realized she was sinking. *(beginning to cry)* She was sinking because she'd lost so much blood and the water was so cold down there at the bottom of the well that she was passing out. My little Lotty was going to *sleep in the cold and the dark AND ALL I COULD DO WAS STAND THERE – SURROUNDED BY MOVIE STARS WITH A DRINK IN MY HAND – AND WATCH HER SLIPPING LOWER AND LOWER…INTO THE WATER…YOU SEE EVERYTHING WAS FROZEN BUT HER! SHE WAS DROWNING AND I COULDN'T DO ANYTHING BUT IT WASN'T MY – (suddenly slumps, drained)* It was my fault. *(filling with rage)* My baby was slipping into the cold black water and crying for her mama and her mama couldn't do anything because her MAMA WAS TOO DRUNK TO WAKE UP FROM HER STUPID DREAMS!!! TOO DRUNK TO MOVE!!! Too drunk to hear my baby crying for me to save her.

CIGARETTE GIRL. *(hugging* **EVELYN***)* Oh honey, I – I don't know what to say. I – Let me get you a cold cloth, and maybe a drink of water. I'll be right back, I promise.

(**CIGARETTE GIRL** *leaves.* **EVELYN** *looks back at the frozen figures in the darkness.*)

EVELYN. This is a frozen moment...like the dream...

(*SFX: We hear a child's voice, crying and calling out in ghostly whispers.*)

CHARLOTTE. *Mama...Mama...It's cold, Mama...*

EVELYN. Lotty? Lotty, is that you?

CHARLOTTE. *Mama...Mama...It's dark...*

EVELYN. I know, baby. Mama knows.

CHARLOTTE. Help me, Mama.

EVELYN. *(beginning to cry)* I can't, sweetheart. I can't. Mama's in the frozen moment...

CHARLOTTE. Mama...hurry...please...

EVELYN. Mama's in her dreams and she can't get out...

CHARLOTTE. I'm sleepy, Mama...

EVELYN. ...And she's so sorry, baby. *(weeping)* My little Lotty...Mama's so sorry... (*The rest is said as it was heard in the voice over at the top of the show.*) It was mama's fault...it was all mama's fault...if only she could have –

CHARLOTTE. *Mama...please...*

EVELYN. *(sobs and wails)* ...no NO *NO! My baby! No...*

CHARLOTTE. *Mama...*

(*Keening,* **EVELYN** *looks around, and seeing the knife she lunges toward it.*)

EVELYN. If I can break the frozen moment...

CHARLOTTE. I don't want to sleep, mama...

(**EVELYN** *picks up the knife and stands, steadying herself against the table.*)

EVELYN. It's okay, baby. Mama's coming.

(*SFX: The chorus of whispers as heard at the top of the act building quickly to a crescendo.*)

CHARLOTTE. *I'm cold Mama...so cold...*

(**EVELYN** *raises the knife...*)

EVELYN. *Mama's coming, Lotty! Hold on!* She just has to get out of this dream first…

(**EVELYN** *takes a deep breath, her hand drawing back that extra bit, preparing to drive it into her own chest. But even as she does…*)

(blackout)

(SFX: The whispers reach a peak that holds for a moment and then, as before abruptly cut off. Silence.)

End of Act 1

BEFORE ACT 2 BEGINS...

*(An amusingly catty or "bitchy," **PRODUCTION ASSISTANT** – or **P.A.** – enters the lobby near the end of the Intermission to recall the "Extras" back into the theatre, where shooting of the movie they're working on will resume shortly. NOTE: The text below provides a framework for what must, of necessity be at least partially improvised to cover the interaction with audience returning.)*

P.A. O-*KAY EVERYONE! Guess what?* Break's over so get your underpaid but over-fed Extra-butts back in the theatre. Let's go. Let's go! LET'S *GO!* After *countless* setbacks, the crew is apparently all but finished with the exterior stuff and wants to move inside next. Who knows? We're only three hours *behind*…you may yet be allowed to go before the sun comes up. Okay…Keep it movin'. Back to your seats… *(to a very casually or very formally dressed patron)* Oh excuse me, sweetie…I mean, I *KNOW* this movie isn't *exactly Oscar-bound…* – I mean, *come on! Who do they think they're kidding with a title like "Curtains: The Phantom of the Theatre II"? – But* still…you are *supposed* to be at the "the-a-tre." Are you telling me that's what you would *honestly* wear if you were going out to a *real* play? *(whatever the response…)* Okay…fine, *fine! Yadda Yadda!* Keep it moving! Keep it moving. *(shouting after them as they pass)* Just don't sit in the first row!…or six! *(to another patron with similar attire "issues")* Oh, don't *you* even *start* with me, Mister. You're not exactly Henry Higgins at the Opera yourself, you know. *Henry Higgins?* Hel-*lo? "Pygmalion"? "Shaw?"* Try *reading* a book sometime. Oh don't give *me that look!* It has been *far too long* a day for *that.* Just get back to your seat. *(shouting across the lobby at a straggler)* HEY! You there! I think you can afford to abandon the *donut* table for awhile. It'll still be there when you get back. Extras! I swear! Now go! GO! *GO!*

(As soon as the **P.A.** *begins to herd the audience back into the theatre,* **IAN**, *the film production's Accountant strolls onto the stage, cell phone in hand. NOTE: As with* **P.A.** *above, the text below provides a framework for what must, of necessity be at least partially improvised while the audience is returning to the house. He finishes up as the* **P.A.** *comes down to the stage to begin Act 2.)*

IAN. *(in a bad mood)* Yes…Ted Warberg's Personal Assistant plea – NO! Don't put me on hold! Hello? *Hello? (waits on hold)* …Hello? Yes I am *still* holding…for Ted Warberg's Personal Assistant, Tina, yes. I – …Of *course* she's there, can you put me through to her extens – …I *don't care* whether *you've* seen her there today or not I'm sure she's – …You normally see everybody who comes in do you? That's fascinating, um, what's your name again?…Katrina?…With *two* "*t*"*s*…and a "y" instead of an "I," I see. Well – NO! Don't put – *(waits on hold)* …Oh good. You're back…Yes, you *did* already say you see everyone who comes in and – …Katrina… *Katrina? KATRINA with two "t"s and a "y"!* Let me ask you something…what time did you start work today? A couple hours ago.…Right. Well, Katrina, I don't know if you *know* this or not but sometimes *other* people start work much earlier than you do and *that* might be why you didn't see her come in. So will you just patch me through *please?…Thank you…*Sure. You too. *(waits while phone rings)* Please not voice mail not voice mail not – *TINA!* It's Ian. Is Ted there *nodon'tputmeonhold! (waits on hold)* …Hi Tina… *(suddenly annoyed)* Why are *you* picking up this line? Yes *she* put me on hold. And if she comes back and finds me not there I'm going to have to go through all of this again! And *if* I *do…*I promise you Katrina, with two "t"s and a "y" that I will have you in the unemployment line so fast it'll make your head spin! Thank you. *(waits on hold)* TINA! Please *don't put me on hold! Ted wanted me put right through on his personal cell when I called…*Because he wouldn't give me the number. Thanks.

ACT 2

Scene One

"SOLILOQUY"

*(Once the audience is back, **P.A.** moves back into the theatre and down to the stage, where **JIMMY**, a young stagehand is assisting a **SET DRESSER,** and **IAN** is on his cell-phone pacing impatiently back and forth. As **P.A.** approaches, **IAN** walks upstage to make his conversation more private.)*

P.A. *(to the audience, as he approaches the stage)* Thank you all for cooperating…and *please* once we start shooting *no changing seats. (to* **JIMMY***)* They *are* coming in now aren't they?

JIMMY. That's what Jackie said.

P.A. Please tell me you got a second opinion.

JIMMY. Well I –

P.A. *Please* tell me you didn't just have me round up the entire *herd* on the say-so of the Queen of *Denial.*

JIMMY. She seemed pretty sure they were done out there and ready to come inside.

P.A. Oh *please. She's* also pretty sure that her hair *doesn't* frighten children. That doesn't make it *true. (to himself) God I need a cigarette.*

SET DRESSER. You're not allowed.

P.A. *I know! I know!* I'm not allowed to smoke in here.

SET DRESSER. You shouldn't smoke *at all!* It's a disgusting habit. *And* it's like forcing the rest of us to smoke along with you!

P.A. *(takes out a lighter and a pack of cigarettes and fixes her with a stare)* Do you have any idea how many people are still *alive today* because of *the calming effect* these things have on me alone?

SET DRESSER. If you want to kill yourself, fine…

P.A. *A hundred and six.*

SET DRESSER. Do it outside…

P.A. …And that *doesn't* include the *idiot* who almost *ran me off the road* on the way here – he would be a hundred and seven – or *you,* right now.

SET DRESSER. Yeah? Well, don't kill the rest of us by doing it in here.

P.A. You *have* noticed that there's a *city* out there, haven't you? Smog? Cars? Smoke stacks? You breathed *all* of *that* on your way here!

SET DRESSER. All the more reason not to have to breathe anymore *crap* because of you.

P.A. *(takes out a cigarette) A hundred and eight.*

*(Enter **ACTOR**, stage left, with a bottle of water, looking for assistance. He approaches **P.A.** from behind and taps him on the shoulder.)*

ACTOR. Excuse me –

P.A. AHHH! *(spins to face **ACTOR** and struggles to recover from the scare)* Oh – my – GOD!

ACTOR. Sorry. I just –

P.A. *Oh, too late, my friend!* You're a hundred and *NINE!* *(to* **SET DRESSER***)* That's it. I'm on break!

SET DRESSER. Whatever.

*(Exit **P.A.**, stage left.)*

P.A.. *(offstage)* Hundred and *nine…*

*(**ACTOR** watches **P.A.** go then turns back as **IAN** strolls downstage, still on the phone.)*

IAN. I don't think that's the *point,* is it Ted? He's *over!* That's all I'm saying…Well, what did Cyrus say? Is he gonna float this or not?

(ACTOR tries to get IAN's attention as he draws near.)

ACTOR. Excuse me…

(IAN looks right at him, then does an about face and heads back upstage, becoming inaudible again.)

IAN. That's not an answer, Ted…Neither is that…Listen… Ted…it's *very simple…it's a Yes or No kind of thing…*

SET DRESSER. Can you get me… *(some item appropriate to what she's working on)*

JIMMY. Sure.

(As he turns towards stage left **JIMMY** *sees* **ACTOR** *for the first time.)*

Can I help you?

ACTOR. Yes! Thank you. When I got here they told me they were running *way* behind so I went into my trailer for a bit of a nap. Anyway…it was more of a nap than I planned but nobody'd come to give me a call so…I thought I'd better find out where we're at. *Oh…*sorry. My manners. I'm Sven.

(They shake hands.)

JIMMY. I'm Jimmy. *(beat)* Uh…we're still running *late,* for sure. I know that. But I *did hear* they're just about ready to move inside. So, we should be getting to your stuff before too long.

(Enter **ANIMAL WRANGLER***, stage right.)*

WRANGLER. Excuse me! I don't want to "freak" anybody here but ummm…. has anybody seen a big black rat out here?

SET DRESSER. A black rat?

WRANGLER. *(nods)* Yeah. About *yea* long… *(indicates a large rat)*

SET DRESSER. And you *don't know where it is?*

WRANGLER. They. There's five of them.

SET DRESSER. *FIVE?*

WRANGLER. Don't panic! My assistant's gone to the can. I haven't had a chance to see if he just brought in one of the empty cages by mistake. I just wanted to check out here first to be safe. *(to the audience)* Don't worry folks! If you feel anything moving around your feet could you just call me please? They like to stick to the corners and follow the walls so most likely only you guys on the sides would see them. If you do… *Please…*DON'T SHOUT OR MAKE ANY SUDDEN MOVES! Of course, they're perfectly tame and there's no danger…but it's still best *not* to scare them…or tick them off. Thanks for your cooperation.

(Exit **WRANGLER.***)*

ACTOR. *(to* **JIMMY***)* So everything's running smoothly here then?

JIMMY. Hey. You know what they say, dude: S.N.A.F.U. Situation Normal…All Fu –

ACTOR. Yes! Yes. I've heard the phrase. *(looking around)* I guess there's no chance I'm at the wrong location is there?

JIMMY. *(smiles)* Nope. This is *it*. In all its *ancient* glory. They keep saying they'll tear it down and build a new one but they never do.

ACTOR. It *has* been here awhile.

JIMMY. You're telling me. My Dad's *oldest brother* worked here as a tech like…I don't know…30 or 40 years ago or something. I can't remember exactly. It was whenever that fire was…you know, the electrical one that took the top off the place. I know he worked here then 'cause that's what made him quit. Apparently he had a thing for the actress who was killed in the fire. And the theatre's main tech guy, Phil Something-or-other, who also died, was like, one of his best friends.

ACTOR. I hope they've fixed the wiring since then?

JIMMY. I wouldn't count on it. *(studying the old man)* You look familiar for some reason. I've been here for a few years. Have you ever worked here before?

ACTOR. *(absently)* Oh I've worked here before… *(beat)* A very long time ago. *(to* **JIMMY***)* Before your time. A *very* long time ago. Probably even before your *ancient* Father's *even MORE ancient* brother's time.

JIMMY. *(smiling)* That long ago, huh?

ACTOR. *(smiling back)* Oh yeah. *(to* **JIMMY***)* Will I be in anyone's way if I just walk the stage a bit? This is where most of my stuff's being shot.

JIMMY. Knock yourself out.

(Exit **JIMMY***, stage left.))*

IAN. *(coming back downstage)* Okay…*Okay*, Ted…Thank you. Decisions are always appreciated…Of *course it won't be your neck!* I promise I'll take full responsibility. I'll tell them to send half the crew home when the scheduled shift is up. Then we're only dealing with minor overs… Well, Ted, that's why you pay me the big bucks…Ha. Ha. Very funny. Catch you later.

*(***IAN*** hangs up and exits left.)*

*(Throughout this, ***ACTOR*** has been strolling across the stage, gazing about. Now he pauses to touch some permanent fixture with nostalgic fondness. Smiles. Sighs.)*

ACTOR. Home again. Home again. *(beat)* Long time coming. *(looks out and up towards the ceiling of the house)* Finally got me back here didn't you? Or did you? You wouldn't wait this long for little old me would you? After all this time?

*(Enter ***JIMMY*** carrying the same stained Ouija board found in the first scene.)*

JIMMY. Hey! Look what I found? A Ouija board!

*(***ACTOR*** reacts to this with dread, which swiftly turns to resignation. He sighs.)*

SET DRESSER. *(to* **JIMMY***)* I didn't *ask* for a *Ouija* board.

*(***ACTOR*** shakes his head a little and smiles. Looks back at the same point in space as before.)*

ACTOR. I should've known.

JIMMY. *(to* **ACTOR***)* You ever seen one of these?

    (**ACTOR** *turns to regard* **JIMMY***.*)

ACTOR. Oh yes. I've seen *that one,* in fact.

JIMMY. This one? This particular one?

    (**ACTOR** *nods.*)

How can you tell?

ACTOR. That stain. I was there the night that happened.

JIMMY. What is it? Coffee?

    (**ACTOR** *shakes his head.* **JIMMY** *looks at the board again.*)

    (*Enter* **TERRY***, the director and* **IAN***, left.*)

TERRY. This is *bull,* Ian. *Bull!*

IAN. No Terry…it's *finance.* You're gonna go over on this thing.

TERRY. By what? Huh? A few grand?

IAN. More like a hundred grand.

TERRY. Oh *please!* They'll spend more than *that* on the commercial for the next Schwarzeneggar movie…

    (**IAN** *opens his mouth to speak.*)

…*JUST* to *air it!*

    (**IAN** *opens his mouth again.*)

…*ONCE!* So don't give me the inflexible bean-counter routine. This is personal. It's Ted tugging on the leash again.

IAN. You know Ted would never –

TERRY. Of *COURSE* he would. And if he wouldn't *you would!* Well, fine. Take half the crew. I can do it in fewer shots. There's always another way around it.

IAN. That's what I like to hear.

TERRY. Oh *is it,* Ian? Is it really? You see, I kind of figured that'd make you nervous. You forcing me to *improvise! Ooooo! Or even worse – dare I say it? – be CREATIVE!*

IAN. Look, Terry, I know how you fe –

TERRY. *(dead serious)* Don't finish that sentence, Ian. Not if you want us to go on comfortably *pretending* we're friends. You have no idea how I feel and you *never will.* *(bitter)* It's not your fault. It's just something people like you and Ted *lack.* You want to tell me I have to work *around* that lack of yours, or Ted's, *fine!* But *don't* ask me to help you pretend that *I'm the one* who's missing something here. Now, if you'll excuse me, I have work to do. At least I will…when my *half-crew* finishes striking outside and finally gets in here so we can make use of all these good people *(indicates the audience).* Before you tell me I have to send *half of them home! (without missing a beat, turns to* **ACTOR** *and continues)* You're here! Thank god! Something's finally gone right today.

ACTOR. One of those days, hmmm?

TERRY. Aren't they all? Listen, are you okay to hang around longer than scheduled? I'm supposed to get to you next but the bottom line will be friendlier if I get rid of as many people as fast a possible.

ACTOR. No problem. I'm here 'til you're done with me.

TERRY. My God! A work ethic. I didn't know they were still making those.

ACTOR. *(joking)* Shhh! Not so loud or everybody'll want one.

TERRY. Well, I doubt that. *(beat)* So, since we have some time to wait… *(notices* **JIMMY***)* What's that?

JIMMY. Just something I found backstage. He says it's a piece of this place's history.

TERRY. Well, put it back. And *make sure* somebody sees it *after* we're gone. *Then* if you want to take it, fine. You're on your own. It's your job. But I *promised* both the manager *and* the local theatre group that *nothing* would go missing while *my people* were in here.

ACTOR. I doubt that board would go missing no matter what. In fact, I'd bet that even if our young friend here *tried* to take it with him…it'd find it's way back.

(**TERRY** *just stares.*)

JIMMY. You think this is blood don't you?

ACTOR. I *know* it's blood. Three layers of it, in fact.

JIMMY. Okay…this I *gotta* hear.

ACTOR. *(with a look at* **TERRY***)* Well…I don't want to hold things up here…keep you from anything.

JIMMY. I work for the theatre. I was off-the-clock hours ago.

TERRY. *(shrugs)* I've got time. But I warn you…if it's good I'll steal it for my next horror flick.

ACTOR. If you want it, it's yours. You'd be doing all the work anyway…I'm not much of a story-teller unless it's written down for me. But I can give you the facts.

(They pull up some chairs or boxes to sit on.)

I first saw this board on October 31, 1937…just before the war. But it was stained with blood long before that. It originally belonged to a fellow by the name of Merlin Black, a rather infamous, magician and escape artist of the day. He was born March 25, 1874. The same day as Houdini. He was found on October 31, 1926 – the day Houdini died – lying across his Ouija board with his throat cut. *(pointing at the Ouija board) That* Ouija board.

TERRY. Suicide?

ACTOR. *(shrugs)* That's what some concluded. They thought he was distraught because the manager of this theatre had canceled his Halloween show for October 31, 1926 and booked another magician in his place. Others saw it differently, as more of…a test.

TERRY. A test?

ACTOR. A test of his beliefs, his knowledge of the occult. A test to see if what he had come to believe was possible was in fact possible.

JIMMY. By cutting his own throat?

ACTOR. Well…the thing he wanted to test, to find out…was whether or not he could come back from the dead. *(points at the Ouija board again)* …Using that.

TERRY. And how was *that* supposed to help him come back from the dead?

ACTOR. *(reciting)* "The blood of four into the board. / The First one through reaps the reward. / The second must therein remain, / To feed the First with meat of pain. / To the whisper'd call of the First, / childless mother comes…Death's chains to burst./ Thus freed the First in spirit waits/ 'Til recall'd by Unbeliever's blood…back through the parting gate." That was the only message they found…the only one he left.

TERRY. Well…if he was trying to make his living as a poet, it's no wonder he killed himself.

ACTOR. Anyway, Black swore he would maintain his hold on this world, through the Ouija board, and that by reaching out from beyond the grave, through the board, he would bring about his own resurrection.

TERRY. I wonder if he started rethinking that little scheme when he realized he was just going to die and that was it.

ACTOR. Who says he did? You have to remember, Black wasn't just a performing magician who wanted to keep living. He had studied and *believed in* Magic, *real Magic,* his whole life. It was his *religion.* And he had been just as obsessed with the idea of conquering Death. Not just because he wanted to go on living as an ordinary mortal, but because he believed that anyone with the will and…well, I guess, the *power* to return would come back changed somehow. More powerful maybe. Possibly immortal…who knows? But it's quite an act of faith when you think about it.

TERRY. So you don't think he's dead?

ACTOR. Ah! But that's not really the interesting question is it? *Of course* he's dead. But is he closer to coming back *now* than he was after his death in '26? *That* as the man said, *is the question.*

TERRY. *(scoffs)* Ha! I doubt it!

ACTOR. Why? Don't you think it's just possible someone… maybe only a very special person, could ever be so determined to remain in this world that they could maintain their grip on this life, and eventually pull themselves back to it, even after death?

TERRY. No. Well…unless it was my ex-wife's lawyer and he'd figured out a new way to get money out of me.

ACTOR. Well think about this…Black held hopes of finding a way to return. And in his final days some say he believed he'd found the formula. Think of his final note as the plan…the *recipe* for his resurrection… "The blood of four into the board…the first gets their reward" Well, Black was definitely the first and we know what reward *he* would want.

TERRY. Okay…but where's he going to come up with three other *volunteers* who don't mind *dying* just to help him come back so he can try and outdo David Copperfield in Vegas?

ACTOR. Who said they had to volunteer? Or even be willing? I don't think they were and I saw it happen. On October 31st, 1937, when Presto tried to contact Merlin Black through *that* Ouija board on a live radio broadcast.

JIMMY. Oh *man!* This is *too cool!*

TERRY. What are you saying?

ACTOR. Just that two people *died* that night while in contact with Black's Ouija board. The first of them was the *same* theater owner who had canceled what Black had intended to be his "Farewell" performance, October 31, 1926. Halloween. He died, for real, in front of a theater full of people, right over there. *(points to the place where the board was set up in the first scene)* What better person to "feed" Black the "meat" of his "pain"?

TERRY. How did he die?

ACTOR. Well…*technically,* he died of a heart attack.

TERRY. Well, there you go then…According to the *bad poetry* his *blood,* the "blood of the "second" would have had to pass into the board. A heart attack wouldn't do that.

ACTOR. Ah…but before he had the heart attack, what probably *caused it*…He was *attacked* by one of the other volunteers onstage. He had his face smashed into the board and his throat cut.

TERRY. What?

ACTOR. *(nods)* Right over the board. There was plenty of blood. And then, that same night…while everyone was trying to save his life and get his attacker under control, the *third* – a woman, selected from the audience at random – stabbed herself and died bleeding over the board…A woman who had lost her only daughter in a tragic accident just a year before. A "childless mother" in other words. That only leaves a fourth to allow Black to make his return.

TERRY. Yeah. Sure. Well, you'll forgive me if I doubt that one more stain on that board will mean anybody's coming back from the dead. Only Jesus, John Travolta, and Burt Reynolds can do that.

ACTOR. *(laughs)* True. True. But what if Black gets the fourth? Jesus returned more powerful than before…he *had* triumphed over Death after all. And what did he do with that power? He ignored the lure of Dominion on Earth and opened the gates of heaven, of salvation for all mankind instead.

JIMMY. And everybody thought Travolta was dead but he came back with *"Urban Cowboy"* and *"Blow Out!"* And Burt made *the "Bandit"* movies AND *"Cannonball Run"*

ACTOR. Well…I rest my case. And with all this evidence of the awesome powers of those who return from the dead…my question is this: What if Black is not quite so…*selfless* and *benign as Jesus was?*…Or as, I'm sure, *John* or *Burt* are for that matter?

TERRY. *(laughs)* You'll forgive me if that question doesn't keep me up at night, I hope?

ACTOR. *(holds out the board…)* And why should it? If you want to know for sure all you have to do is…well, I'm sure I've got a penknife here somewhere…

TERRY. Without me you don't get a paycheck…

ACTOR. *(laughing)* Good point. I withdraw the suggestion.

TERRY. So you really believe in this supernatural stuff?

ACTOR. *(shrugs)* I don't know. But I would like to believe the world is a little more mysterious, a little deeper than what we see on the surface. Isn't that why we tell stories? To try and touch the mysterious truths that lie beneath it all?

TERRY. Only if our market research is *completely* wrong… which, for the sake of our box-office on *this little gem* I certainly hope it's not.

ACTOR. Oh. So what's this picture about then?…According to your market research?

TERRY. It's mostly about young people with ridiculously lean and trim bodies wanting to have sex with each other.… And then *having it.* Of course, lots of them die horribly as one grotesque horror after another attacks them in their dreams but…at least they *look good* right up to the end. All of the girls – except the heroin – have to get naked or at least topless at some point…*naturally.* We *do* have the video-rental market to consider. *(shakes his head)* Oh yes! And it's also about things *exploding!* If the commercial doesn't have at least *one* explosion these days they'll label you a *drama* and then it's game over. *(beat)* Anyway, it's been good talking with you but I'd better go see how things are coming along outside.

(Exit **TERRY***, left.)*

JIMMY. You have to forgive, Terry. He's not as cynical as he makes it seem. He wrote this really beautiful screen-play – I mean *makes-you-cry* beautiful – and he's been shopping it around for ten years. But the studios won't touch it.

ACTOR. Why not? If it's so good?

JIMMY. Money. These slasher flicks cost next to nothing to make and they always turn a profit. His make the most. They're not going to let him start making "real" movies anytime soon. It's not in their best interests.

ACTOR. Oh.

JIMMY. Of course, that doesn't stop them from dangling it like a carrot every time they want him to sign on for another teenie hack 'n' slash. So tell me more about this show you saw where everybody dies?

ACTOR. Not much to tell. People started dying…I threw it back to the network and we went off the air right away.

JIMMY. You were *working* on the show?

ACTOR. I was the announcer. *(beat)* "Good Evening, Friends. And Welcome. I'm Corwin Haygood and do you know what? It's *Eight O'Clock!* It's *Saturday Night!* It's *Prime Time Variety Time* on WKBS, brought to you by your good friends at *Silver Fox! Silver Fox,* fast-becoming everybody's favourite smoke. That's because only *Silver Fox* is formulated to satisfy your F-Zone. That's *'F' for 'Flavour'* and *'F' for 'Fast'!* Nothing gives you *great taste* and *real smoking satisfaction* swifter than a fox, *except…Silver Fox!* The one that comes in a silver box. So remember friends: When it comes to *your* smoking pleasure…only *Silver Fox…satisfies!*"

JIMMY. Corwin? I thought you said your name was Sven.

ACTOR. It is. *(shrugs)* Corwin sounded better…at least I always thought it did. But then, after the war, when the mood of the country changed – and people like that pig-eyed bastard McCarthy started looking for Reds under every bed – suddenly anybody who used a stage name was immediately suspected of having something to hide. So I dropped mine…to show I had nothing to hide. My career went with it. Nobody particularly cared that Iversson wasn't even a Russian name. It was like…it was like the whole country became *children* overnight…afraid to walk down a certain street because one of the bigger kids had told them there was a mean-old junkyard dog off his chain down there. Nobody bothered to check on the big kid's story. They just…decided not to visit people who actually *lived* on that street for awhile.

JIMMY. So what did you do after that?

ACTOR. I went back to the stage. Toronto. New York. Montreal. Chicago. The stage was safe by then. Movies and television were reaching people in the *millions*. So, naturally, the powers that be couldn't care less about what some idiot in tights and a fake beard might have to say to a hundred people in a basement. *(beat)* After awhile things got back to normal but by that time radio was dead. So I kicked around Los Angeles picking up what commercial work I could, and a few low-budget horror flicks.

JIMMY. Oh my god! *Iversson!* *"S"* Iversson. *You're S. Iversson!* You were in *"From a Curséd Tomb"* and *"Stage of Blood and Shadows"*!

ACTOR. *(laughs, remembering)* Oh yes. Which the producers in their infinite wisdom renamed "From the Wings of Death" for its release – they always wanted everything to be *"From"* something. *"From* the Black Crypt," *"From* an Unquiet Grave," *"From* an Alien World." Never understood that – Of course, everybody thought it was going to be yet another vampire flick so they either stayed away from it or were disappointed by it.

JIMMY. But it's a *classic!* It's like…my favourite horror movie of *all time!* Well…*after* "The Changeling" and "In the Mouth of Madness" anyway.

ACTOR. Mmmm, well, it's in good company then. I like both of those.

*(Enter **P.A.** at left, crossing right, slowing to listen in on the conversation.)*

JIMMY. And it was definitely the most powerful Anti-McCarthyist movie ever. Even more than *"Invasion of the Body Snatchers."*

ACTOR. Well…it had the advantage of coming out *after* McCarthy. It's easy to take a stand once the opponent's left the ring.

JIMMY. It was still pretty cool. And you were *amazing* as Sir Anthony Drake.

ACTOR. Thanks. You're very kind.

P.A. *(gasps and crosses to* **ACTOR***) YOU* were Sir Anthony *Drake? (another gasp) OH my GOD!* I *hated you!* You scared me to *death* in that movie. I didn't sleep for *a week,* swear to god.

ACTOR. I guess I did my job then.

JIMMY. Are you *kidding?* You should have gotten the *Oscar* for that role. I mean it. That speech you gave at the end? You know…after you told the guy who was supposed to be Senator McCarthy that the drinks had been drugged. And then you made them listen to you perform a speech from a play they'd banned?

P.A. *Oh yeah!* I remember that! And all the while the fire you'd set in the basement was feeding on the stacks of banned scripts, building until it consumed the *whole theatre. I swear I was crying at that point.* That was such a powerful moment.

ACTOR. I think the writer thought it was too. I always thought it was a little *heavy-handed.*

JIMMY. Can I ask you something?

ACTOR. Sure.

JIMMY. The last shot of the film…The one that was super-imposed over the image of the burning scripts?

ACTOR. Now that *was* a great effect. And much cheaper than burning down the actual theater.

JIMMY. Anyway, we only get to hear the first part of your speech before the helpless screaming of the audience and the roar of the flames drowns it out. After that I could only make out a word or two. I was wondering, were you really saying anything there? I mean did you have a real speech memorized for that and everything?

ACTOR. Oh yes. And I *loved* giving that speech too. It was the biggest, hammiest, most over-the-top moment of my career and I *loved every second of it.* Unfortunately, the director said I got it right on the first take so I only ever got to say it once. I always regretted that. Usually in movies you have to do everything a hundred times. But the one time I would have *loved* the repetition…

the director says "Cut. Print it." And "Let's move on."
I always wanted to do it in front of a real audience,
just once. Maybe on a talk show or something. But the
chance never came.

JIMMY. Do you remember it?

ACTOR. Oh yes. I never forgot it.

JIMMY. Well, I feel like a geek asking this but I'm gonna ask
it anyway…Could you do it now? For me?

ACTOR. *(looking around)* Well, I wouldn't want to disturb
anybody while they're working…

P.A. Oh, believe *me*, honey. All we're doing here is waiting. And I'll bet *they'd* love it. *(looks out to the audience)*
Wouldn't you guys? *(beat) HEL-LO?* Anybody out there
in Extra-land? We've just asked a veteran performer
of stage, screen and *honest to God Old-Time Radio (gets
a look from* ACTOR*)* to perform his favorite speech of
all time! How about a little *encouragement? (He starts
applauding and if necessary continues to goad the audience
until they join in.)*

*(ACTOR stands to address the audience, humbled by
their applause.)*

ACTOR. Thank you. That's very kind.

(He gestures to silence the applause.)

P.A. Okay! He *said* "thank you!" You can all *shut up* now! *(to
ACTOR)* You have the floor maestro.

*(Enter the ANIMAL WRANGLER at the back of the house
and moving down the aisle looking for something that
might be around people's feet.)*

ACTOR. Okay…well, if we're going to inflict this on *everybody* I'd better explain it a little. As some of you might
have heard, I have been asked to perform the final
speech of that "classic" horror-movie "Stage of Blood
and Shadows"…also known, unfortunately, as "From
the Wings of Death."

WRANGLER. *(shouting)* Excuse me! Sorry to interrupt!

SET DRESSER. It better not be about rats on the loose!

WRANGLER. It's not. They were in their cage. He'd just brought the wrong one in.

SET DRESSER. Good.

WRANGLER. Yeah. *(beat)* Has anybody seen a snake?

SET DRESSER. WHAT?

(**WRANGLER** *resumes moving down the aisle looking around peoples' feet.*)

WRANGLER. Wait! THERE HE IS! *NOBODY MOVE! (forces his way in amongst the crowd bent over as though trying to catch the snake)* Okay! Got him! *(Stands upright holding a wriggly snake and inadvertently shaking it in the faces of those he's trying to reassure as he makes his way back out to the aisle.)* Everybody just relax now! It's all under control. *(to* **ACTOR***)* Sorry for the interruption.

ACTOR. That's okay. *(beat)* Well…I don't know how exciting this will be compared to *that!* Or how well it's going to work out of context but…well, nothing ventured, nothing gained. So, with your indulgence, I'd like to set this up for those of you who *haven't* been fortunate enough to encounter this "classic" bit of cinema on the late late show over the years…

(picks up his water bottle)

The story was inspired by the McCarthy-era political "witch-hunt" that went looking for Communists under every bed in the United States and destroyed a lot of careers…a lot of *lives* in the process…particularly of people in the entertainment business. The character I played was Sir Anthony Drake, a noted actor and playwright whose life and sanity were ruined by a Conspiracy-obsessed Senator named Joseph McCready – well, nobody ever said it was a subtle piece – At any rate, as the film goes along, Drake takes his revenge on those of McCready's agents who were directly responsible for the deaths of his wife and child – among other things – by befriending them, luring them to his theatre and killing them off one by one.

(takes a sip of water)

ACTOR. *(cont.)* By the time a fairly determined detective named Harrison is beginning to close in on him, Drake is the toast of McCready's elite and he invites all of them to attend a *private* premiere of his brand new one-man show, a tour-de-force work inspired – he says – by McCready himself. McCready is flattered and makes sure that every one of his supporters is in attendance. The first act portrays McCready and his kind as heroes fighting for Truth, Justice, and the American Way. Needless to say…They love it. At the intermission it's free drinks for everyone…and as this is a night for paying tribute to McCready there are many toasts. So everybody drinks.

(raises his water bottle in a toasting gesture and drinks)

Meanwhile, backstage, Detective Harrison thinks he's caught up with Drake at last. But he hasn't even guessed the half of what Drake's up to. Now, Drake likes Harrison. He respects him and tries to get him to leave voluntarily…

(shakes his head)

Unfortunately, Harrison isn't dismissed so easily. There is a struggle, a fight in a room filled with banned and censored scripts and books…. a room filled with flames… And it's impossible to tell who's got the upper hand…… And then we see the crowd have returned to their seats, ready for the curtain to rise on the second act.

(moves his chair down center)

There is a pause. A hush falls over the crowd. The curtain doesn't open. Reaction shots from the audience beginning to wonder what's taking so long. Still the curtain remains shut. McCready nudges the man beside him and says, "I guess he's building the suspense, huh?" He laughs and looks back at the curtain. He doesn't notice the way the man barely heard him…or the confused, concerned look on the man's face as he stares at his own hand, flexing and curling the fingers. And then…just as the crowd begins to murmur, agitated…the curtain rises. A hush falls once more.

(sets his water on the floor, sits in chair)

ACTOR. *(cont.)* And there sits Drake, staring straight ahead. He doesn't say anything. He just sits there, staring ahead…glancing occasionally at his character's ever-present pocket watch…while the crowd becomes agitated once more. And staring at them. We see their reactions change from patience…to expectation…to exasperation. One of them tells his wife he's going out for a cigarette. She doesn't look at him or acknowledge that she's heard him. And that's when he realizes…he hasn't the strength to lift himself out of his seat. With a tremendous effort he lifts one arm an inch or so off the arm rest of the chair and then it flops back down again. Out of the corner of his eye he can see his wife's eyes darting about panic-stricken, but everything else about her is frozen. Still. He asks what's going on. First quietly, to himself. Then louder, demanding, frightened. Other voices join his. We see, from his point of view others struggling weakly in their seats, futile attempts to escape. And their voices get louder…AND LOUDER. Turning to panicked, guttural sounds as even the ability to speak fails. We see McCready himself, struggling, panicking…and then his eyes lock with Drake's. It takes him a moment but he finally puts it together. "YOU DID THIS!" he barely manages through a slackening jaw, saliva flying. If he could point an accusing finger he would. But he can't. And a frightened tear rolls out of one eye as he settles back in his seat, unable now to even struggle… unable to do anything except watch as Drake *(mimes this)* Checks his pocket watch once more…closes it… returns it to his vest pocket…And rises to address his captive audience…

(He rises and steps forward. **JIMMY** *moves down in front of the stage so he can see better.)*

JIMMY. *(as he crosses down)* This is *so* cool.

ACTOR. Ladies and Gentlemen, gentle listeners all. I welcome you to this Final Act. I trust and can see you are all much refresh'd by your recent intermission and though you have indulged in *far too many* self-congratulating toasts, I can see that I have your undivided attention as well. That is, of course, because you have been drugged. You find you cannot move, not even to turn your head. You find it difficult even to blink. I can assure you this state is only temporary. It is followed by darkness. I know that thought must comfort you. You are all so *fond* of *darkness.* So fond of obscuring shadows that cloak your deeds. So fond of *the dark night* when the "good things of day begin to droop and drowse," when your "black agents to their preys do rouse." Now I know this listening must be difficult for you. You prefer to talk, to make speeches, to accuse, and accuse again and before they can deny, or explain or even draw breath to speak *accuse again!* Until the *accusation* is all that matters! Until the list of *alleged crimes* has been trumpeted so loud and so long that none but the *most vigilant* would even *think to consider* whether these charges have any substance. Yes…all this listening must be quite new and terrifying to you, mustn't it? It might even be making you long for the darkness that even now you know is about to fall. But I'm afraid you will have to listen a little longer. And I'm afraid that I intend to talk to you – *not* about darkness at all. No. No. – but about *Light.*

(Enter **TERRY** *at left.)*

Ah…Light! There really is so much of it it makes you wonder how anyone ever got the idea to *dismiss* the virtue of the Light, and the Light of Virtue, and believe instead that there might be, in darkness, any *real* power. How did they come to look up into the night sky and say "See there! A vast blanket of darkness, an endless void that threatens to swallow a scattering of lights no bigger than pinheads. How fragile is the Light. How overwhelming and powerful the Darkness." How? Well the only thing that I can think of is that they were afraid of the darkness. Looking as they did, with eyes whose sight was distorted by a lens of fear, they saw the darkness and were afraid of it. And being afraid of it, they gave it power over them. And giving it power over them…they sought to serve it. *(laughs a slightly crazed laugh to himself)* Ah…the poor misguided souls. How to tell them the truth? How to help them see the message right before their very eyes?

*(**ACTOR** throws his arms wide, shouting.)*

ACTOR. *(cont.)* *WERE ALL THOSE TINY LIGHTS OF HEAVEN EXTINGUISHED…ALL OF THEM…SAVE ONE…STILL THERE WOULD BE LIGHT! AND WERE ALL THOSE TINY LIGHTS OF HEAVEN EXTINGUISHED…ALL OF THEM…SAVE ONE…STILL THERE WOULD BE…NO DARKNESS!* Shadow is only Light's way of saying "See the brightness first. See the important and obvious first! *Then* examine the secondary things to understand their place and reason for being." How to give them this truth? That there *is no darkness*…except in their own hearts? How do the Virtuous help them to, as Milton would have it, "see to do what virtue would by her own radiant light, though sun and moon were in the flat sea sunk?" How to make them understand that "He that has light within his own clear breast may sit in the center and enjoy bright day…" while "he that hides a *dark soul* and *foul thoughts…Benighted* walks" though it be "under the midday sun"? How to do this? By telling them *stories.* By giving them dialogues, pantomimes, farces, tragedies, ballets, operas, all these worthy vessels, and a thousand more, filled to overflowing with the speculations, the hopes, and the fears of people much like themselves, and by holding all of these things up to the *LIGHT!* *(gazes about him at the stage lights and closes his eyes, basking in the glow, as in a trance)* The light…The light… *(suddenly, snapping back into himself)* But stories don't give answers, though they might seem to, to the unaccustomed eye. No, that is not the job of the artist or the entertainer. And why?

(He looks out at the audience, questioning.)

ACTOR. *(cont.)* …Because, in the end, we are not moved by Answers. Answers do not motivate, inspire or guide us in our journey. No. They don't. *That* is what *Questions* do. And that is why we tell each other stories. Time and again. Over and over. Not for the illusory answers they might seem to offer…but for the *very real*, profound and *simple* questions they help us dare to ask. For the questions they help shape in our minds. Questions, not answers, Senator. *Questions* are the light we shine ahead of us, into the future, into the unknown, into that *supposedly* fearful darkness *which does not exist!*…so long as we are willing to shine our light into it…and to oppose those who would see that light extinguished.

(He fills with rage, reflecting.)

(upset) My friends…so many of them, gone. *(pointing at the Senator, accusing)* BECAUSE OF YOU, SENATOR! AND YOUR KIND! BECAUSE OF YOUR FEAR! YOUR FEAR OF THOSE WHO POSSESSED THE COURAGE YOU NEVER HAD! THE COURAGE TO FACE THE QUESTIONS KNOWING THAT EACH ANSWER ONLY LEADS TO MORE QUESTIONS! AND THE COURAGE TO FIND COMFORT IN THAT KNOWLEDGE. You took their livelihoods, destroyed their families, alienated them from their communities…even had them killed…all in the hope that you could silence their voices. You tried to extinguish their light as petty tyrants always have. And you failed. Just as petty tyrants always have. For *I* have saved their light. You see? I saved their words and their light. And although you cannot move you can no doubt smell the smoke by now…and feel the heat rising through the floor! Oh yes, Senator! I saved their words but what good are words without breath to carry them? Or tongues to shape them? So I gave them back their breaths that they might speak to you. And I gave them

back their tongues that you might understand them clearly! Can you smell the smoke, Senator? Can you feel their hot breath! They have something to say to you! *Let their passionate words fuel tongues of flame and blaze to the HEAVENS, Senator! Let them set your eyes ablaze with their questioning fire that even in your dying moments you might know…THE LIGHT PREVAILS! THE LIGHT PREVAILS! THE LIGHT PREVAILS!!!*

JIMMY. Oh *yeah!!!*

(**P.A.** *and* **JIMMY** *applaud wildly, inciting the audience to do the same if they're not already.*)

ACTOR. *(recovering himself, humbled, laughing, moved)* Thank you. Thank you. All of you. I guess you know why they cut it short now. Definitely a wise move. But thank you…for making an old actor's dream come true at last. I never thought I'd live to see the d —

(**ACTOR** *looks suddenly unwell. Gasps in pain and reaches over his left shoulder with his right hand to press where it hurts.* **JIMMY** *rushes across to him.*)

JIMMY. Are you alright? Sven? *Sven?*

ACTOR. *(unsteady on his feet)* Yes. Yes, I'm fine. Just need to sit down for a minute.

(**P.A.** *crosses to pick up Actor's water bottle and offer it.*)

P.A. Here…you should have some water!

JIMMY. Should we call for an ambulance? You're not having a heart attack are you?

(*He helps* **ACTOR** *sit down in chair again.*)

ACTOR. *(shakes his head, recovering as the dizzy spell passes)* No. No. I'm fine. *(takes the water)* Thanks. *(settles back on the chair)* It's just a muscle spasm. Probably from the commercial I shot yesterday. *(a big exhale)* Well…I guess that's what I get for spending the whole day *pretending* to suffer from intense shoulder pain.

P.A. Oh, that *happens!* A friend of mine spent a morning playing Migraine sufferer #1 and came down with an *actual* migraine that night…*AND he'd NEVER had a migraine in his life!*

ACTOR. *(joking but looking weak)* And who says acting isn't tough? Which way's the nearest men's room? I'd like to splash a little cold water on my face.

JIMMY. It's off that way. *(pointing off right)* Do you want me to go with you.

ACTOR. No. No. I'm fine. Thanks though.

TERRY. *(crossing to touch **ACTOR**'s arm)* Hey…I just want to say that was…*amazing*. Truly amazing.

ACTOR. Hey…what've John, Burt, and Jesus got that I haven't got?

*(Exit **ACTOR** stage right.)*

*(Enter **WRANGLER** stage right. He moves towards center, and stands there hands on hips, eyes searching the air over the heads of the audience. Everyone looks at him. He shields his eyes and continues to look.)*

WRANGLER. Has anybody seen a bat?

SET DRESSER. *WHAT?*

(A fake bat is flown over the heads of the audience.)

WRANGLER. *(pointing)* There it is! Right there! *NOBODY MOVE! And DON'T MAKE ANY NOISE! It's – (looks more closely)* Wait a minute. That's a *fake!* Oh…very funny Jack. *(beat)* I hope the real one bites you!

*(Exit **WRANGLER** stage right.)*

*(Enter a **SCRIPT GIRL**, left. She is crying.)*

SCRIPT GIRL. *(between sobs)* Terry…the ambulance guys want to talk to you?

TERRY. What ambulance guys?

SCRIPT GIRL. The ones we called when we found – I thought you knew… *(is overcome)*

TERRY. Found what? Knew what?

SCRIPT GIRL. He was so nice…and happy…and energetic… I didn't know…I should've known but I didn't…

TERRY. Known what? Lisa, what the hell are you talking about?

(Everyone draws closer to hear.)

SCRIPT GIRL. *(between hitching breaths and sobs)* …Okay…I'm gonna get a grip…I mean it's not like I knew him it's just…he was so nice…he reminded me of my grandfather…

TERRY. Lisa *please…*

SCRIPT GIRL. The old actor…Sven Iversson…he arrived and we talked for awhile and when he found out how late we were running he asked if there was somewhere he could lie down for a quick nap…He said he'd been on his feet all day…but he didn't want me to let him sleep for more than half an hour…But I *did! I forgot!* And then about twenty minutes ago I remembered but when I went to check on him, he was – *(can say no more)*

TERRY. Lisa…if you're trying to tell us he was dead, somebody's played a *very mean* joke on you. He was just here. Not two minutes ago.

SCRIPT GIRL. What are you talking about? Terry… The ambulance guys tried to get him back but they couldn't. They declared him dead and put him in the ambulance ten minutes ago. I watched them do it.

(Everyone is looking at everyone else except **SCRIPT GIRL.***)*

SCRIPT GIRL. What…?

(blackout)

(SFX: Whispers as from Act 1 build to a crescendo and cut out when…)

Scene Two

"HAPPY HALLOWEEN"

(**JENNA BREMMEN**, *a real estate agent, attempts to open the doors at the back of the house. We hear her muttering as she fumbles with a batch of keys at last entering the dark house with only a small, key-chain flashlight to make her way. She is clutching her briefcase under one arm and is talking on her cell phone. She makes her way down to the stage.*)

JENNA. *(as she struggles through the door)* Yeah… Yeah… Yeah, uh Martin? Could you hold on a sec?… *(turns on the flashlight)* …Okay… I *know you're not here*. Even though *this* is where you *said you'd be*, where you *promised you'd be?* … Yeah yeah. Okay. "Meeting ran late" sure… You know it doesn't matter if you're lying or not. The point is I'm a gorgeous, sexy, female real estate agent walking around *all alone* in a big, empty, creepy old theater at the *exact* time in history when the news is reminding us *hourly* that gorgeous, sexy, female real estate agents *should not* be walking around *all alone* in big, empty, creepy old theaters! That's how you end up one of those people on the Six o'clock News, Martin. You know the ones I mean? The dead ones? The ones who die doing something that in hindsight they had no business doing so everybody figures they got what they deserved. I – …Don't interrupt me when I'm ranting, Martin. The point is: *I'm NOT one of those people.* I *don't* deserve to be raped and killed in some empty old building, not *just* because *nobody deserves that*, but also because *I* actually went to the trouble of arranging a macho-male chaperon to keep me safe… Yes, Martin, that *was* supposed to be you. Only *you're not here, are you? You're* – Where are you anyway? Are you going to be here *soon* at least? …Oh god! You're not even close. *(She gets up onto the stage.)* …Well at least stay on the phone with me. And don't bitch to *me* about your air-time. It's the least you can do for *letting me down like this.* ...Good. I'm glad you see it my way. ...Well, stay on the l – What? ...Are you going under hydro lines or something? I – Martin? *Martin? (sighs, annoyed)* Great! *(She hits speed dial and waits.)* Ooooh! *(hangs up and tries again)* Get *off the phone you idiot... (muttering)* ...So I can get you ON the phone and tell you what an idiot you are! *(angs up again)* Okay! Fine! Desert me in my hour of need. See if I care. Now... where the hell are those lights?

(Exit **JENNA**, *and her flashlight, stage left.)*

JENNA. *(cont.)* Come *on! OPEN! Stupid thing.*

(We hear the sounds of her striking something metal.)

(SFX: Whispers cut in at a steady, strong level.)

Hello?...Hello? Is somebody out there? Just a sec...

(We hear a breaker thrown offstage and the stage working lights come on to reveal the stage is a mess. Littered with old or broken bits of scenery and equipment. Upstage, some tall piece of furniture is covered with a black cloth and so blends almost completely with the blackout curtains.)

(SFX: Whispers cut out.)

(Enter **JENNA**. *She looks around at the mess, moving upstage, her back to the audience.)*

What a dump.

(SFX: whispers)

*(***JENNA** *turns, eyes searching out over the house for the source of the sound.)*

(SFX: Whispers cut out.)

Okay, I did *not* imagine that.

(Her phone rings. She jumps and gasps, startled. Then answers it.)

JENNA. *(cont.)* Jenna Bremmen…Oh. It's you…. No, I'm *not* alright…. *You were supposed to be here.* That's what's wrong…. No. Nothing's happened. I just thought I heard something…. NO, I don't know what it was. I guess I can't even be sure I heard it. Could've been the wind. I don't know…. No, I *don't* really think it was the wind. It *sounded* like a whole bunch of people *whispering,* only it *can't have been,* because I'm pretty sure even I would notice a whole crowd of people sneaking around here whether they were whispering or not…. No…No!…Because it *can't be. There's no equipment* for anyone to be *playing around* with, that's why. The techs have spent the last month stripping this place of everything that *wasn't* nailed down and of *almost everything* that *was….* I guess they plan to install a lot of it in the new thea – Hello? Hell – …Oh. There you are. Is your battery dying?…Well can't you plug it into the cigarette lighter or something?…I *don't know!* So that you can hear me screaming for help so you'll know when to call the police and tell them where to find the body.

(SFX: Whispers start again.)

Oh my God! I can hear that sound again. Like a crowd of people whispering. *(beat)* Can you hear it at your end?…Are you sure?…Oh right, you're in a car on the highway. Well, it's loud and clear over here…

(Stage lights flicker and go out.)

Oh god…. the lights just went out.

(Lights come back up to no more than half their original level. And now, the clown magician who performed in the lobby before the show, clearly the apparition of the late Merlin Black, the **JUGGLER,** *is standing up center next to the black-draped piece of furniture. He is staring at* **JENNA,** *a wide eyed look that exaggerates the creepy/menacing effect of his grease-paint mask. She remains with her back to him, oblivious.)*

JENNA. *(cont.)* ...*Oh!* It's okay...they're back again. But I can *still* hear that noise...Well, of course it's weird. But it *is* just a noise...*You* don't like it? Try *being here. Which you were supposed to be,* I'd like to remind you!...Why don't I *what?* Did you *really* just ask why don't I leave?...Because I have a client coming, that's why. Because if I don't *see* my clients I find it very hard to convince them of the merits of buying an old dump like this, that's why. In case you've forgotten, *that's how I make my living...* Well, yeah it *is* like that. But you're forgetting a couple of things.

(The **JUGGLER** *begins to approach* **JENNA** *very, very slowly from behind.)*

First of all, the reason people in horror movies *don't* leave the creepy old house as soon as something seems *weird* is because A) They don't *know* they're a character *in* a horror movie, so they do the things that normal people would do if they were in the same situation. And B) If *normal people* just *ran away* every time something *unexpected* happened to them, they'd get *fired* from their jobs and be no fun at *surprise parties....*

(The **JUGGLER** *is only a few feet behind her.)*

I don't *care* what *Eddie Murphy says.* He was joking. If you're one of those people who're always sitting there in the audience thinking that a *character* in a *movie* should somehow *psychically know* that there's something hiding in the closet or sneaking up behind them then *you're* the *idiot...*

(The **JUGGLER** *is almost upon her, he reaches out, one hand on either side of her head...and the lights begin to flicker.)*

(looking up) Oh for crying out loud! *Not again...*

(The **JUGGLER** *closes his eyes and leans his head back as the lights go out completely.)*

(SFX: The whispers cut out with the lights.)

(Silence for at least five seconds.)

(We hear Jenna's cluster of keys strike the stage.)

JENNA. *(cont.) You have got to be kidding me…*It's pitch Black and I dropped my keys…My flashlight is *attached to my keys… (gets on her knees to hunt around for them)* Where are you? Where are you?…No, Martin, not you. My keys. Ah. Here they are…

(**JENNA** *turns on her flashlight and exits left to get the stage lights on again.*)

No, I'm fine, Martin…it's just the lights. The lousy electrical is just one of the many *charms* of this place. It caused half the place to *burn* about 25 years ago or so. Killed two people. Too bad it didn't just level the place so they could have built something *useful* in its place… Like what? Well, right *now* I'm thinking *like a bar.*

(We hear her strike the breaker box, and the lights come on again.)

(The **JUGGLER** *is nowhere to be seen but up center, where he first appeared, the Ouija board is propped up against the blackout curtain.)*

(Enter **JENNA**, *left.)*

(Sighs as she enters.) …I'm fine. I swear. It's just, all those stories in the papers and on the radio lately. They've got me spooked, that's all. I – *What* – Looks like I'm losing you. So listen: Get here as soon as you can, okay? I'll wait for you if I have to but you are buying me a drink or five to make it up to me. Okay? Martin? Hello? Did you get that? *(hangs up)* You better have.

(**JENNA** *looks at her watch, sighs, then starts looking around again.*)

Come on, Mr. Fox. Let's get on with it.

(For the first time, she notices the Ouija board. Considers for a moment whether it was there when she looked a couple minutes ago. Then curiosity gets the best of her and she walks toward it. Then, just as she is bending forward, reaching towards it…the blackout curtain suddenly billows out towards her and an arm reaches through for her.)

(*JENNA* *screams and leaps away as an elderly man,* **THOMAS FOX**, *at last finds the gap in the curtain and enters up center. The Ouija Board remains forgotten on the floor.*)

THOMAS FOX. I'm sorry! I'm so *terribly sorry! I didn't mean to frighten you!*

JENNA. Well you did a *great job* for *not trying*. Who are you?

THOMAS FOX. I'm Thomas Fox, Ms. Bremmen. I'm here for our appointment. *(beat)* You *are* Ms. Bremmen, aren't you?

(*JENNA* *nods.*)

Yes. I was pretty sure. I recognized you from your picture on the signs around town.

JENNA. *(recovering)* Well, that's good. I'd hate to think you made of point of scaring the heck out of people you don't recognize.

THOMAS FOX. Really. I *am* very sorry. I *can't say* how sorry I am. I know this must be a stressful job already and with all this horrible news in the papers lately…those poor women…well, I imagine the *last thing you need* is some old man leaping out from behind a curtain at you.

JENNA. I'd have to say you're right there.

THOMAS FOX. I hope we can still conduct our business…

JENNA. *(laughing it off, with an effort.)* Of course. *(extends her hand)* Let's start again: I'm Jenna Bremmen.

THOMAS FOX. *(shakes her hand)* Thomas Fox. Pleased to meet you. I'm sorry again for startling you. I arrived a little early and tried knocking on the front doors but then it occurred to me there was probably a back-entrance to an office or something. So I went around the side and tried the door. It was open so I came in thinking you must already be here. There was a flashlight by the door so I took it and went down. Unfortunately… it died on me while I was down there. Had a hell of a time finding my way out.

JENNA. The door was *open?*

THOMAS FOX. Well, it wasn't actually *open.* Just unlocked.

JENNA. If I've told those tech-heads once I've told them a thousand times… *(huffs, annoyed)*

THOMAS FOX. It was probably an accident.

JENNA. Yes. The second one this week. *(beat)* Well, anyway. There's no harm done – except to my blood-pressure – so shall we take the tour?

THOMAS FOX. Well, actually…Ms. Bremmen…Jenna… *(steps toward her)* I'm not really here to see the facility.

JENNA. *(steps back, nervous)* I'm sorry?

THOMAS FOX. No. It isn't necessary, you see. I'm quite familiar with this building.

JENNA. Oh. *(relieved)* You've seen a lot of shows here?

THOMAS FOX. *(nods)* Quite a few, yes. Over the years. *(looking around)* I even worked here, backstage, front of house for a few years in my teens. Of course, *that* was a *very long time ago.*

JENNA. *(putting on her charm)* Oh come *on.* The *Eighties* weren't *that* long ago.

THOMAS FOX. *(chuckles)* Would those be the Nineteen or the Eighteen-Eighties? *(beat)* Actually, Ms. Bremmen, I worked here more than *fifty years ago.* Of course, *(acknowledging her flirtation)* I won't say how many more than fifty. A man should *never* reveal his age on a first date. *(with a wink)* Spoils the mystery.

JENNA. *(relaxing more)* Well, we wouldn't want to spoil the mystery would we? Now, Mr. Fox, if you didn't want to look around…

THOMAS FOX. Well, actually I *did.* I just meant I didn't need the official tour.

JENNA. Oh. Well, you'll forgive me for being blunt, Mr. Fox but are you actually interested in purchasing this building?

THOMAS FOX. In all honesty…no, Ms. Bremmen, I'm not.

JENNA. I see. Well then, if you don't mind, Mr. Fox, I have a lot of other calls to make today. So if you don't mind…

(She begins to exit left but he grabs her arm.)

THOMAS FOX. *NO! PLEASE! Ms. Bremmen…hear me out.* This is *more* important than a sales commission.

JENNA. Please let go of my arm, Mr. Fox.

THOMAS FOX. If you promise to hear me out.

JENNA. Please let go of my arm, Mr. Fox.

THOMAS FOX. Of course. *(lets go)* Of course. I'm so sorry. This is just so important…you have no idea. If you could please spare me just ten minutes of your time? I can at least *guarantee* you'll have an interesting story to tell.

JENNA. And will I also know why you've wasted my time when you never had any intention of buying this building? The conclusion that leaps to my mind has to do with the stories in the news lately…

THOMAS FOX. *(gasps)* No! NO! I'd never…I mean, I'm not… *(runs one hand through his hair, messing it in the process)* …Hmmm. That's a good point. How do I assure you I'm not some killer rapist? That *was* stupid of me. Maybe if my niece had come with me…Look, all I can say is, frankly, Ms. Bremmen, I'm a very old man. I –

JENNA. Please, Mr. Fox. Don't. It's alright. I'm here anyway, and a friend of mine should be arriving any minute. A *male* friend of mine. I asked him to join me today *because* of those news stories.…*Of course, he's late.* But I'm going to gamble I could fend you off until he gets here.

THOMAS FOX. I have no doubt you could, Ms. Bremmen.

JENNA. You have ten minutes. Go.

THOMAS FOX. Very well. I don't suppose there's any chance you've ever read the book "Our Stage In History."

JENNA. Did Stephen King write it?

THOMAS FOX. No.

JENNA. Then I haven't read it.

THOMAS FOX. It's not surprising. It was never a big seller. But I've always felt it was the most important book I ever wrote.

JENNA. You're a writer? I'm sorry I didn't –

THOMAS FOX. Oh, that's alright. I made a very good living for myself, writing a lot of different things, under a lot of different names – *None of them were Stephen King, unfortunately,* but – well, I did more than alright. But the book I just mentioned was my most important, I think. To me, at least. To everyone else it was just a local history as seen from the boards of this very theatre and a handful of others like it. But it was *this* theatre and what happened here a long time ago that drove me to work here, to learn everything I could about this building and the people who had passed through it and of course to write about it.

JENNA. I'm not sure where you're going with this, Mr. Fox, but I'm not sure you're going to get to your point in ten minutes.

THOMAS FOX. Yes. Of course. You're right. I've just lived with all of this so long, examined it so thoroughly, it's very difficult to know what I can leave out and still make you see its importance. But I'll try to be direct. When I was a child my father appeared on this stage, not as a performer but as a volunteer picked from the audience during a live radio broadcast. This is back when radio was the…the Internet of its day, I suppose. I'm not completely sure of that…I write with a computer now but "going online" is…well, it's not my thing.

(*JENNA taps her watch.*)

Of course, of course. The performer featured on that show was a psychic called *Presto,* he was the uh… "Amazing Kreskin" of his day. He wanted my father and two others to use a Ouija board to help him "make contact" with the spirit of a deceased magician, a fellow with a fairly sinister reputation by the name of Merlin Black, also known as, The Juggler. The Ouija board they used – you know what that is?

(*JENNA nods.*)

THOMAS FOX. *(cont.)* The board had belonged to Black before he died. At any rate, that night, on this very stage, while he was in contact with this Ouija board… my father, a quiet, gentle man who rarely raised his voice and *never* raised a hand in anger…my father who certainly *didn't believe* in Ouija boards or even hypnotism…cut the throat of a man he had never met before.

JENNA. Oh my god.

THOMAS FOX. He was institutionalized for the rest of his life. Which wasn't as long as it might have been as he killed himself while in hospital. But that was quite a few years later. I had grown to be a young man by then. But before he died, my father told me an incredible story. It was a story just packed with details – factual details – that it was *extremely* unlikely he could ever have known. I won't try to convince you of both the strangeness and the truth of the things he told me. It would take too long. The most important thing is: He believed – and with good reason I came to think – that someone, some…*thing* had possessed him that night. He believed that thing was *evil*. And he believed that it was trying to get back into this world. He believed that thing was the undead spirit of *the Juggler, Merlin Black.*

JENNA. Mr. Fox, I may be a Stephen King fan, but I should tell you I enjoy spooky stories because *I don't* believe they're possible or likely to come true. They're safe. Pure fantasy…

THOMAS FOX. I know. I know. And of course they are. But what I'm telling you, Ms. Bremmen, what a lifetime of research – research I couldn't show you in ten *hours,* let alone ten minutes – has *proven to me is true,* is this: My father was right. Merlin Black *was* trying to come back from the dead…and he's still trying. Now wait! Please don't say anything. I know how this sounds. But let me tell you why I'm here and then with the moments I have left, I can hopefully tell you enough of what I've learned to convince you to help me.

JENNA. To help you what?

THOMAS FOX. Destroy this place.

JENNA. What?

THOMAS FOX. *(urgent, rushing.)* Or something in this place. Something that is keeping Black's power, his spirit alive. Please bear with me, Ms. Bremmen. These are facts, things you can verify: The date of the broadcast, when my father…did what he did…was October 31, 1937. Black died on October 31, 1926, the same day as Houdini.

JENNA. Houdini?

THOMAS FOX. They were born the same day you know: March 24, 1874. They were professional rivals for years. But near the end they were enemies. Something Houdini apparently said. Do you know the story of how Houdini died? A student from McGill punched him in the stomach. It seriously injured him and he died from complications. Some said Black was behind it. Others that it was a devotee of Black's, a girl who used the pseudonym "Fille de Noir" – *"Daughter of Black"* – who sent her boyfriend to do the job. She was one of a…a *cult* I guess you'd call it that believed Black could and would come back from the dead. He was to be their *dark Messiah!*

(pacing now)

This is coming out all wrong. I know. It's confused. The web is so vast the details seem unconnected.

JENNA. Mr. Fox….

THOMAS FOX. That same day, Black died by his own hand. He cut his throat and bled to death over his Ouija board. In his hand he clutched a piece of paper, the only message he left behind. It read: "The blood of four into the board. / The First one through reaps the reward. / The second must therein remain, / To feed the First with meat of pain. / To the whisper'd call of the First, / childless mother comes…Death's chains to burst./ Thus freed the First in spirit waits/ 'Til recall'd by Unbeliever's blood…back through the parting gate."

JENNA. Mr. Fox…

THOMAS FOX. Don't you see? Black *believed he could die and come back again, using the Ouija board.* He also believed that he would come back, transformed somehow, more powerful, more than mortal. The "first," *Black,* would get his "reward" of renewed life. The "second," a man he had reason to hate, was the one my father killed. He, my father, spoke as though he *was* Black as he was doing it. Many who had known Black or had seen him perform were there that night and they swore it was *Black* and not *my father* who wielded the knife. Whoever it was, though, he cut the man's throat right over the Ouija board. The third, the "childless mother" was also there that night. She killed herself over the board as well.

JENNA. *(getting nervous)* I'm sorry, Mr. Fox. I really don't see how I can help you and I really do have to go.

(She tries to leave but he grabs her arms and won't let go.)

THOMAS FOX. No! Please! You *have* to *listen to me!* Don't you see? The blood of the fourth was never spilled upon the board but it's *STILL HERE! WAITING!* People have seen it over the years, playing with it, not knowing what it was. Some have even admitted to taking it away with them. But then…they can't find it again. They assume they lost it and forget. But years later another story of more people who've seen it, found it AGAIN, RIGHT HERE, in the Orpheus…people who've *held it…USED IT!* Don't you *understand!?!* IT'S LOOKING FOR THE *FOURTH!* AND IF IT FINDS THEM THEN *THE JUGGLER IS GOING TO RETURN! HE WILL BE LOOSE UPON THIS EARTH WITH UNSPEAKABLE POWERS.*

(SFX: whispers)

(The lights flicker and dim.)

JENNA. *LET ME GO! LET ME GO!*

THOMAS FOX. I *CAN'T!* You must help me find the board. *I HAVE TO DESTROY IT! IT'S THE ONLY WAY WE CAN KNOW FOR SURE!*

(blackout)

*(**JENNA** screams. There is the sound of a body blow and a gasp from **FOX**. We hear a body hit the floor and **JENNA** moans as though in pain.)*

*(Lights flicker dully back to life for an instant to reveal **THE JUGGLER** up center again. **FOX** is down center, clutching his abdomen. **JENNA** is lying on the floor, groaning, she tries to lift her head but passes out. The lights continue to flicker.)*

*(between gasps, to **JENNA**)* I'm so sorry, Ms. Bremmen...I never meant to...Are you alright?

*(The **JUGGLER** moves down, closing in behind **FOX** who is unaware of his presence.)*

*(SFX: Whispers get louder as the **JUGGLER** nears **FOX**.)*

Ms. Bremman?

(blackout)

(SFX: After several seconds, the whispers crescendo then cease.)

*(Lights up to half to reveal **JENNA** lying as she was before and no sign of **THE JUGGLER** or **FOX**. The Ouija board is lying where Fox was.)*

*(Enter **MARTIN**, left.)*

MARTIN. *Oh my god! Jenna! JENNA?*

(He kneels by her and raises her head. She stirs.)

Please, Jenna please! Tell me you're alright.

JENNA. *(groggy)* I'm...fine...I...think...

MARTIN. What happened? Did you faint or something?

JENNA. No he...he...

MARTIN. Who? There's no one else here, is there? I – Oh my god. *You're not saying you were attacked? Are you? Is someone else here?*

JENNA. He's…

(She looks around for Fox, confused by his disappearance.)

He was right here. He…he was crazy…babbling all this stuff about possession and Ouija boards and coming back from the dead. I thought he was going to kill me…

MARTIN. I don't *see* anybody.

JENNA. I'm telling you he was here. I'm not making this up.

MARTIN. Of course not. I never said you were.

(MARTIN gets up to look around, spies the Ouija board and picks it up. He carries it back to JENNA and kneeling down, up stage of and slightly behind her holds the board in front of her for her to see.)

What's this?

JENNA. Oh my *god! That's…*I think that's what he said was looking for. Of course he probably left it here himself. To make his story more believable.

MARTIN. *(sets the board down in front of her)* What? You mean you don't believe in ghosts and Ouija boards?

JENNA. *(rubbing her head)* Of course not. I believe there are *crazy people…*Ow! *(wincing) That's* going to be a bump.

(Lights flicker and dim again.)

(SFX: whispers, very loud)

(blackout)

Okay! *WHAT IS GOING ON HERE?*

(Lights up and there is **THE JUGGLER** *up center again and moving slowly down right. His crazed stare never leaves* **JENNA** *who gasps, recoiling into* **MARTIN***'s arms in terror.)*

Oh God! *(points at the* **JUGGLER***)* It's him! *Martin! It's HIM! IT'S HIM! (looking to* **MARTIN** *who is smiling, calm.) MARTIN IT'S – (suddenly, catching on)* Oh…my…god.

MARTIN. *(smiling, innocent)* What?

JENNA. The sound effects…the old man…this clown-faced guy…This whole thing's been a *setup* all along!

MARTIN. Don't be ridiculous.

JENNA. *(turning her head to look at him as best she can)* And *YOU* did it! *Didn't you?* You set this whole thing up! You *JERK!*

MARTIN. *(mocking indignance)* What? You think that I would go to all this trouble for some kind of…some kind of Halloween *prank?*

JENNA. I can't *believe you did this!*

MARTIN. *(disappointed)* So you're telling me you that my friend here *isn't* the ghost of Merlin Black, The Juggler?

(The **JUGGLER** *stops down right, eyes still fixed on* **JENNA,** *his crazed expression unchanged.)*

*Or…*that he's come *back from the dead* thanks to this Ouija board and his Mastery of the *Dark Arts?*

JENNA. Ah-HA! See? If this *wasn't* something you set up yourself how would you *know so much about it?*

MARTIN. *(not convincingly)* A lucky guess?

(She swats at him.)

(trying to be spooky) Or *maybe* I've been waiting for this moment ever since I joined the same mystic cult that *finished off Houdini.* Oooo! Wouldn't *that* be a *scream?*

JENNA. Oh yeah, Martin. You're hilarious. A real *riot!* *(Heaves a sigh, getting over her initial panic. Then, to the air.)* "Laugh?" I thought I'd *DIE!* (beat) Well, for your sake there'd better be a hell of a "Surprise!" coming, you bastard. And it better be followed by a *lot of booze* or I'm going to *kill you.*

MARTIN. *(hugs her, playfully)* Oh…no you won't.

JENNA. *(dusting at her clothes)* If you've messed up my outfit you're footing the bill.

MARTIN. *(chuckling)* Okay. No problem.

JENNA. No problem, for *you,* maybe. *I* nearly had a heart attack thanks to you and clown-boy over here.

MARTIN. *(gasps, feigning indignation)* "Clown-boy?" That's Merlin Black you're talking about there, girly. The greatest sorcerer who ever lived, risen from the dead and awaiting the moment when he will once more become flesh and blood.

JENNA. *(sighs)* No Martin. It isn't. He's probably just some wino you stole from some kid's lame-ass birthday party. Now make with the surprise and tell Bozo over there to stop staring at me.

MARTIN. *(with a look to the* **JUGGLER***)* Well? You heard the lady…

(With sudden, deliberate viciousness, **MARTIN** *clutches a fistful of* **JENNA***'s hair at the back of her head with one hand and shoves up and forward, stretching her exposed throat out over the Ouija board. In his free hand he is now clutching a wicked looking knife.)*

(a glance at **BLACK***)* Sounds like *"Unbelief"* to *me!*

*(*JENNA*'s eyes widen in panic as* **MARTIN** *sets the blade across her throat. We hear her final, sharp, shocked intake of breath.)*

(Blackout as SFX: The chorus of unintelligible whispers build out of the darkness to an unbearable crescendo… then cut off.)

(The rest is silence.)

The End

(…Unless your company or audience would prefer a more amusing, light-hearted ending. In which case…)

ALTERNATE "LIGHTER" ENDING

(SFX: The chorus of unintelligible whispers build out of the darkness to an unbearable crescendo…then is suddenly cut off…By either: HAPPY POLKA MUSIC OR a cacophony of FART NOISES, whichever strikes your fancy to utterly destroy the tension that's been built.)

(Lights up to reveal…)

(JENNA *and* **MARTIN** *in their final horrific freeze, knife at her throat and* **GERALD**…*our director from Act 1, Scene One as he storms down the aisle from the back of the house.)*

GERALD. NO!!! NO! NO!! NO!!! STOP! STOP! FOR THE LOVE OF –

(Sound FX/music cut out.)

PHIL!!!

PHIL. *(offstage) (shouting back)* WHAT!

GERALD. Honestly Phil…Suspension of *disbelief!?! Hmmm!?!* A lingering sense of *dread!?! Terror…?*

PHIL. *(offstage)* What's your point?

GERALD. My *POINT*, Philip…is that these things are SOMEWHAT DIMINISHED when the final rising crescendo of a ghastly undead chorus is abruptly usurped by… *(depending on effect/music used)* …"Uncle Milo's SYMPHONY OF FLATULENCE!!!" (OR……) "The *HAPPY HUN ORCHESTRA'S PERKY POLKA PARTY!!!"*

PHIL. *(offstage)* What are you talking about? The play's over.

GERALD. Over? It's not "over" Phil. It's DEAD. DECEASED. MUTILATED BY YOU AND YOUR COMPLETE AND UTTER INCOMPETENCE!!!

*(***GERALD*** collapses into a huddled sitting position, head in hands.)*

PHIL. *(offstage)* Well…"Dead" is good right? I mean…dead's scary isn't it?

(a muffled whimper from **GERALD***)*

(The actors playing **MARTIN** *and* **JENNA** *awkwardly manage to exchange a look while holding their "freeze" as best they can.)*

JENNA. Uh…Gerald?

GERALD. What?

JENNA. Can we move now?

GERALD. Yes. You may go. Everyone may go. *(sighs and gazes heavenwards)* I KNEW I should have stuck with *FARCE!*

(final blackout)

ABOUT THE PLAYWRIGHT

Born in Toronto, Ontario, Canada, **Todd McGinnis** is a screenwriter, director and award-winning actor and playwright. He is the prolific author of more than 20 full length and one act plays for traditional and alternative venue theatre.

Though he has worked in many genres including horror, historical drama, thriller, and murder mystery, he is best-known for his comedic works: the renaissance-era farce *Knave of Hearts*; his farce set among the gods of Mount Olympus *Thunderbolts and Dunderheads*; the three brothers in a fishing boat comedy *Gone Fishin'*; and his best-selling work *Point of Viewing* about three women co-hosting a live television broadcast gone horribly wrong.

With T. Gregory Argall (*A Year In the Death of Eddie Jester*), Todd has also co-authored the side-splitting comedies *IN-SECURITY: An Alarmingly Romantic Comedy* and *Self-Help for Dummies*.

Todd continues to reside and work in the Toronto area.

OTHER TITLES AVAILABLE FROM BAKER'S PLAYS

A NIGHT OF DARK INTENT

L. Don Swartz

Mystery, Thriller / 8f (2m recorded voices) / Unit Set

Set in October 1978, *A Night of Dark Intent* is the story of six women who spend the weekend together in an abandoned house. The house, however, is no ordidary home: 13 years prior, it was the location of the grisley Stark chillings, in which young Lenora Stark brutally murdered her parents. Now, as the six women try to unravel the secrets of what really happen 13 years ago, they learn a horrifying truth: Lenora Stark as escaped from her asylum and just might be coming home!

From the author of the popular Baker's Plays thiller *Halloween Dreams*, comes a new shrill-inducing chiller, in which six women must race against the clock to solve a murderrnand save their own lives. With a story that thrills, twists, and turns, *A Night of Dark Intent* is the perfect night of theatre for any mystery lover!